THE CHRONICLES
OF HENRY ROACH-DAIRIER:
THE INCEPTION OF
THE COMBINED COLONIES

by Deborah K. Frontiera

ISBN 978-0-9753410-7-0

Library of Congress Control Number: 2004093175

Key words: 1. fiction 2. fantasy 3. insects 4. future worlds 5. young adult 6. adult

The Chronicles of Henry Roach-Dairier:
The Inception of the Combined Colonies
Copyright: 2019, Deborah K. Frontiera

Published by Jade Enterprises
P.O. Box 841654
Houston, TX 77284
713-416-0109

Printed in the United States of America

SPECIAL THANKS

to these professionals:

Cover art by Korey Scott, McKinny, TX

Cover design by Margaret Helminen,
Designotype Printers, Calumet, MI

THE CHRONICLES OF HENRY ROACH-DAIRIER

*Notes of importance to my readers
for a better understanding of this work*

HENRY ROACH-DAIRIER II

I come from a long line of creatures—both ant and roach—named Henry, famous namesakes with already-recorded deeds that make it difficult to walk in their pods sometimes. I resented it as a nymph.

My grandfather, Henry Roach-Dairier, penned the life stories of his ant great-grandfather and great-grandmother—Adeline Harvester and her mate, Henry (now known as the book, The Chronicles of Henry Roach-Dairier:To Build a Tunnel) and then his ant grandfather and grandmother—Henrietta Harvester and her mate, Antony Dairier (which became the volume The Chronicles of Henry Roach-Dairier: New South Dairy Colony 50). When I was near the end of my eleventh season cycle, my grandfather told us his summarized version of the Inception of the Combined Colonies. This occurred over Last Day dinner after I had gotten in trouble for scaring my cousin to tears over fire ant tunnels under Roacheria. That began my fascination with the past. Later, my mother wrote my grandfather's early life after convincing Grandfather to tell it (with my mother using a voice imager) over the course of several Seventhday afternoons. That became The Chronicles of Henry Roach-Dairier: The Re-creation of Roacheria. It was that honesty from Grandfather that convinced me to accept my destiny to continue his mission of promoting understanding between ants and roaches.

To Build a Tunnel and New South Dairy Colony 50 are now required reading in 3rd year Basics in all the Combined Colonies and in our little corner of Roacheria, Meadow Commonwealth, which from its beginning was more like an ant colony than a Roacherian community. I think the day is not far off when my grandfather's early life, The Re-Creation of Roacheria, will also become required reading.

After that Seventhday when my grandfather gave us his synopsis of the Inception of the Combined Colonies, I spent a lot more time with him.

"How come you never wrote a book about the Inception?" I asked.

He laughed before saying, "Between counseling clients, caring for your mother, your aunt, and your uncle, and all the work here in Meadow Commonwealth, there was never a moment to consider it."

"I don't know what to think," I said. "My Antstory book tells about how cruel the roaches were, and how that led to the belief that roaches have no essence. Then I look at my Roachstory account of that time, which makes it seem like some sort of 'great time' for roaches. How can anybody sort out the truth?"

Grandfather was silent.

I continued, "Then, I can't forget when you told us about 'point of view' after that trainer stepped on you for getting the season cycle wrong." For any of my ant readers who are unfamiliar with this ancient Roacherian form of punishment, a roach parent or trainer orders an offending younger roach to lower him or herself into the most humble and humiliating position. Then the parent or trainer—and sometimes a powerful employer over an employee—stomps down as hard as possible on the back of one's thorax, right at the most vulnerable and weak spot where the back of a roach's head plate meets the top of the thorax. I am grateful to say that I have never had to undergo that painful punishment.

Grandfather twitched his antennae in thought before he spoke. "I was fortunate to hear my grandfather's story directly from him. Then I was lucky enough to find old Rex's journal after having Henry, Adeline, and Gabriel's journals given to me. A creature with the patience to search could probably find some records of that time in Roacherian Archives. Your mother's status as a counselor would get you access to those documents, should you be interested. The colonies involved, South Harvester 45, South Dairy 1, and Fire 2, would definitely have records and documents. Often, personal journals are given to such archives and might be available. Anything in Old South Dairy 50 has been lost forever, of course, since the disastrous death of that colony."

We both sighed, thinking about the tragedy of Old South Dairy 50 and the tremendous loss of life the day Antony Dairier, my great-great-grandfather, hatched, when an accident in the science facility sent poisonous fumes through the entire colony.

"But," Grandfather said, looking deeply into my eyes, "someone with great determination might find colony support to search for the truth."

"Are you saying I should write it?"

He shook his antennae. "I would never be so presumptuous as to tell anyone what life work they should choose. Only Essence can answer that for you."

Grandfather left this world the next season cycle, a few days after my thirteenth hatching anniversary. As we gathered to cover him, I listened to many creatures speak about how he had inspired them.

My mother's words last words to him were these: "I promised I would wait, and I have, but now I will publish the story of your young adult life."

My grandmother was too overcome with grief to speak that day, but she talked to all of us many times later about how our grandfather was the most cherished one in her life, and how she never regretted leaving her prominent father's house to join the simple life style of Meadow Commonwealth.

When my turn came to speak at Grandfather's covering, I hesitated. Then I couldn't help what tumbled out. "That story…that truth…I'm going to find it. For you, for me, for everybody. It's too important to leave undone."

Saying a thing is easy. Doing it is quite another matter. I hope I have composed this account up to my grandfather's standards. Because there is as much of a story in the digging—literal and figurative—as in the ancient events themselves, I (unlike my grandfather) have included parts of my own life within the narration of the past. I have included editorial comments as well to help both ant and roach readers understand aspects they might not know.

Like my grandfather, and my mother who narrated his story, I have decided to include here at the onset how ants and roaches came to be the evolved and intelligent creatures we are. Later, you, my readers, will see this again in the context in which Daeira first spoke these words to the members of her colony.

THE BEGINNING:

as revealed to Daeira Dairier
in dreams and meditation

In the beginning, Essence roamed the skies looking for the right place to start a world. She saw that our planet already had cycles of day and night, water and air. It had a set path around its sun so its cycles could be numbered, but it had no life.

"I will see what can live and grow here," she said, and joined herself with it. The Creative Life Force of Essence endowed the waters with miniscule plants and creatures and the cycle of life began.

Essence cherished this new life, but was tired from her journey across the cosmos, so she entered the earth and went to sleep.

Eons later, when she awoke, the planet was filled with life forms. The water and land and air teemed with a great variety of plants and creatures. Some were tiny and frail, others huge and fierce. There was great variety even in their coverings—smooth, hard, scaly, furry. The large, scaly ones dominated at that time.

Essence watched her world. The sun fed the plants, which fed the moving creatures, who then were eaten by larger ones, and on and on. They grew, propagated, and returned to feed the earth when their time was over. Some creatures failed and disappeared, but new ones evolved to take their place.

And ants were there.

Essence, satisfied with the balance and cycles, cradled her world, and went to sleep again.

The pain of many shocks woke Essence. Chunks of matter hurled through the cosmos and struck the planet, killing millions of life forms and knocking the planet in its cosmic path. The dust from their impact screened the sun's light, denying life-giving energy to plants. Essence watched in dismay as thousands of species disappeared from

1

her cherished world. In her grief, she shook. Hills tumbled. Mountains sent forth liquid fire from within.

But even in grief, Essence's Creative Life Force found its way again. An infinite variety of flowering plants came to be. A few species of the scaly creatures and the small ones with fur and feathers survived.

And ants were still there.

Essence watched for many eons as the fur creatures increased in size and began to dominate. "What would happen," Essence said, "if I interfered and gave one life form an advantage? If I gave a tad of my intelligence to a creature, could it create something original, as I have?"

Essence looked closely at each species and finally chose one that seemed different from others. This species was not entirely covered with fur, stood on only two appendages, and had a well-developed nervous system. She infused them with more intelligence and waited to see what would happen.

Season cycles passed. Generations of Duo Pods came and went. Essence saw that they made tools, built things, and developed the planet. Their machines grew ever more complex. Satisfied, Essence took a nap.

Essence awoke with a fever. The planet's surface was a shambles. The air and the water were fouled. All the Duo Pods, all of the feathered creatures, and most of the furry ones were dead forever.

"What has happened to my world?" Essence cried.

Grief for her failed experiment and illness consumed Essence. The earth shook. Storms raged. Her tears covered many lands. Then slowly, the earth healed itself. Although it would take many more eons for all of the Duo Pod creations to return to the earth, the world looked new and fresh once more. Essence found that one substance the Duo Pods had made would not break itself down and feed the earth. They had indeed created something original. Her experiment had not been a total failure.

She looked around hopefully and found that ants, roaches and other insects were not only still there, but had grown greatly in size and changed in other ways.

"Ah, my faithful ants," she said. "You have been with me from the earliest days and have always been civilized. Perhaps the intelligence I gave the Duo Pods was not enough. I will try again. I will give you not only the gift of knowledge, but my compassion as well. And this time, I will not sleep, but will watch over my world. I will be available to my creatures, speaking to their minds when they seek me. When each one's time on earth is done, the part of me that is in them will return to me in unity forever. Eat then, my ants, of the lasting creation of the Duo Pods—plastic—and receive my gifts. Cherish my world and seek to understand its mysteries."

And so we are.

While Essence was speaking, a group of roaches approached. They took the gift of intelligence, but ran away before the second, more important gift of compassion and inner essence was given. Thus they received no more of Essence than had the extinct Duo Pods.

Bemused, Essence observed the roaches as they ran from her. "I must watch and see what comes of this development."

Measuring Time and Distance: My great-great-grandmother, Master Henrietta, the first to understand the writings of the extinct Duo Pods, unraveled some rather unusual things about the measurement systems of those highly-intelligent creatures. While they, like we, found that a season cycle had 365 days an divided those days into fifty-two quarter time frames of seven days each, their beginning of each new season cycle has always seemed a bit odd to me. Their time frames varied from twenty-eight to thirty-one days each, and they had just twelve such time frames. Ours makes much more scientific sense: thirteen time frames of twenty-eight days each, and then Last Day, which is Winter Solstice. It is not part of any time frame, nor is it part of a quarter time frame. Last Day simply is. Then we begin a new year on what the Duo Pods called December 22. Our Summer Solstice Celebration, falling exactly half way through our season cycle, is always the 14th of Seventh Time Frame, with Extra Day falling right before it every fourth season cycle—again not part of any quarter time frame, but simply there. But Summer Solstice fell on what the Duo Pods called June 21. Such important calendar events on completely non-logical days! Lastly, the Duo Pods gave strange names to the days of their quarter time frame: Monday, Tuesday…Our Firstday, Secondday, etc., are ever so much simpler.

The Duo Pod word for h-unit, "hour," was more similar to what we call it, but they had a strange way of measuring distance. A number of f-units, 5,280 to be precise, made up a "mile." Our d-unit is close to that in distance but an even 5,000 f-units. Other Duo Pods used completely different units in 10s, 100s, and 1000s they referred to as "metric." Why didn't they simply use one system? I've asked that of some of our archeologists, but as of this writing, they don't really have an answer.

THE CAST

of Inception of the Combined Colonies:

This list may be important to both ant and roach readers since it involves the present, the past, and several locations. My ant friends often complain that Roach names are so similar, and therefore hard to keep track of, but my roach friends say the same about ant names. I provide here a list so that such confusion might not occur for my readers.

FROM THE PAST:

Daeira.............................Spiritual Guide of South Dairy 1

Dagan and Dailey..........Leaders of South Dairy 50's trade group to South Harvester 45

Dagny ....Spiritual Guide of South Dairy 50

Dahlia.............................South Dairy 50's Council Chief

Dangelis ....Spiritual leader South Dairy 1 before Daeira

Dara ....Young adult female who finds Duncan after his escape

Delana............................South Dairy 1's Council Chief

Dodie and Dart..............Duncan's parents

Duncan...........................Young male ant who escaped South Dairy 1

Fadi ....Fire Ant 2's Commander of the invasion

Faith..............................Fire Ant 2's spiritual guide

Farr................................The fire ant captain who becomes Commander in South Dairy 1

Fauna and Fane..............Fire ant scouts

Fleur..............................Fire ant captain who remains in South Harvester 45 as its first guard commander

Fredrika.........................Fire Colony 2's Council Chief

Hadi ....South Harvester 45's spiritual guide

Hal and Haley ....Mated pair of South Harvester 45 who communicate with Dagan and Dailey and the fire ants

Hesper............................South Harvester 45's Council Chief

Ragnar ....Roach who bought South Dairy 1 from Rainart and who denied all plastic to the ants
Rainart ....First roach who enslaved South Dairy 1
Rand...............................Ragnar's warrior commander
Rashad...........................Rainart's employee, interpreter for the ants
Royce..............................Ragnar's oldest son

My contemporaries:

Daisy ....Chief Archivist at South Dairy 1
Darlene...........................Descendant of Daeira's sister
Gabrielle........................My mother, a counselor of law and only female member of the South East Roach Control Board, governing body of Roacheria
Rabiah ....Descendant of Rainart
Raissa..............................Rabiah's daughter
Rastus ....Descendant of Ragnar

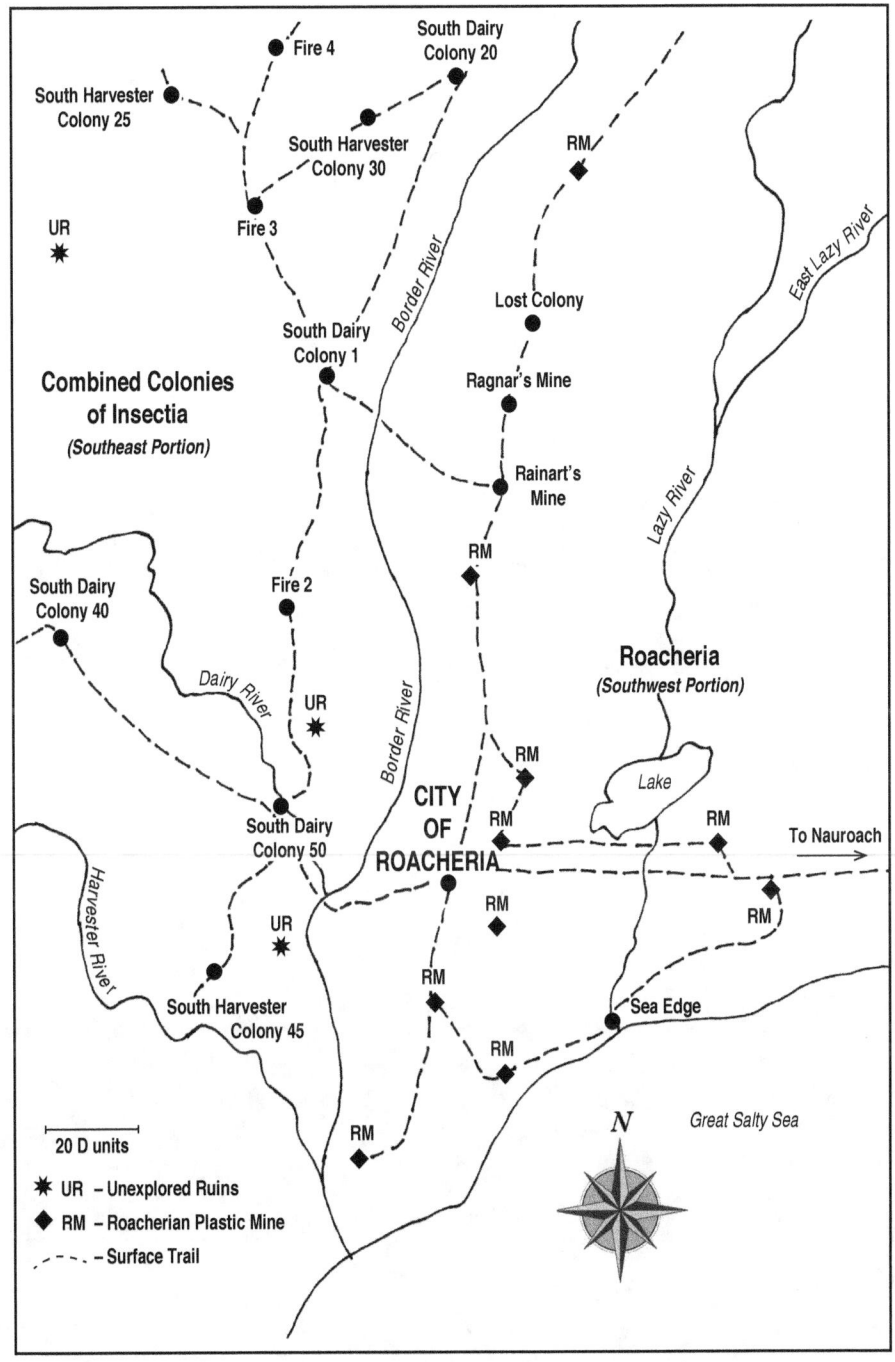

1.

Fourth Time Frame 28, 22 B.C.C.
(Before the Combined Colonies) or 11 O.R.
(Organized Roacheria—as all roaches are taught)

Daeira Dairier rose slowly from deep meditation. She sighed. Being the spiritual leader of her dairying colony had been a blessing when she began. Now it seemed a great burden.

The dream of the previous night had been very troubling. She stood before a gathering of colony members during Seventhday Meditation Service. The tight feeling in her thorax nearly brought on tears. Her expression must have been troubling them; she could feel and smell the worry emanating from their antennae as they reclined on the soft earthen floor of the meditation chamber, silent and solemn. Only a few beeswax lamps provided the faintest glow in the darkened chamber. Perhaps she should not tell them this dream until she understood it better herself. But the last words of the message had been quite clear: "You must prepare them."

Prepare them for what?

While all ants felt the presence of a living spirit deep within them (which they referred to as their essence), not all of them were privileged to hear messages from a "greater presence" they called Essence. Daeira's first dream message had come during her last season cycle of formal training—a time when most young adult ants chose their life's work. It was shortly after the death of their previous spiritual leader, Dangelis, a female who had never taken a mate or had a family, but lived to a very great age helping colony members learn to live in harmony with the natural world and be truly compassionate with each other.

Earlier that morning, Daeira's thoughts had gone back ten season cycles to when her first dream vision had occurred. "I had a beautiful dream last night," Daeira had told her mother the morning after colony members had covered their cherished spiritual leader in the heart of the colony. "I saw a warm, glowing place of peace and light. I saw Old Dangelis among many ants who seemed to shimmer in the glow. I saw Grandmother again, there with Old Dangelis, who told me we should not mourn for her because she was with a great company of those gone before and all was well."

The moment Daeira had stopped talking, her parents had taken her to the Council Chief.

"Our new spiritual leader has been revealed," they had told their leader.

Daeira had been acclaimed as the colony's new spiritual guide, the Voice of Essence, as soon as she described the dream-message to the Council. All the fuss over her had frightened the young female at first, for she was just twenty season cycles old then. Another dream the following night had reassured her that she need not worry about whether or not she was up to the task. Since that day, she had been recording her dreams, telling the whole colony about the care they must show to each other, meeting with small groups daily and larger groups every Seventhday, teaching young adults how to meditate, and showing others how to direct young adults in the way they should live and know Essence.

Daeira, like her predecessor, had also realized she could not serve her colony in the way she had been called and have any energy left for a mate or family. She never asked any male to spend time with her—as she had during her season cycles of job exploration—and politely turned down all invitations that came to her. Young males understood and stopped calling on her.

Now, she faced her colony and said in a shaky voice, "My cherished colony members, a period of very great sorrow will be coming upon us soon. It will test our beliefs and values to our core. But we must support each other, for only in that way will we survive this time of trouble. It might last many season cycles, but we will endure. And when 'soon' is, I also do not know. But Essence will be with us all through it. Of that I am certain."

A thousand questions, all the same, followed. Daeira could not answer them. "I will tell you more as it is revealed to me," was all she could say. Days went by. The initial anxiety was forgotten and life went on in the colony as it always had.

Fifth Time Frame 28, 22 B.C.C.

A time frame later when the moon had completed its phases from new to full to new again, one of the colony messengers taped on Daeira's portal. She put down her writing and let in her visitor.

"Master Daeira, I'm sorry to disturb you, but Council Chief Delana wishes you to come with me to the surface. Two roaches are there and Delana wants your advice as to what to do about them."

Daeira couldn't imagine how her advice would help, for she knew nothing of the roaches who lived several d-units on the other side of a very shallow, slow-moving river meandering along the edge of their colony's meadow area. But as she walked up the tunnel to the surface, the tight feeling in her thorax that she had experienced the previous time frame returned. She stopped for a moment at the colony's entrance. She knew from her previous trips out of the mound that she must let the half-light near the entrance help her adjust to the intensity of the morning sun. Like most colony members, she was more accustomed to smelling her way along the tunnels with her antennae (and writing or reading by the dim light of a single beeswax lamp) than using her eyes in the brightness of the surface.

A fair-sized group of ants stood around one large and one slightly smaller roach standing just outside the main entrance to the mound. The large one was three times the size of any ant. Off to the left, other ants watched over a herd of grasshoppers. Still others were up in nearby trees, tending aphids as they sucked sap from slender tree branches. The sweetness in the late spring air helped relieve Daeira's anxiety. It was a pleasant day, but the heat of summer would soon be upon them. She turned her attention to the group directly ahead of her.

Council Chief Delana addressed her. "Master Daeira, thank you for coming. These two roaches arrived about an h-unit ago, gesturing to our entrance watchers that they wished to speak to someone in charge. We have been trying to communicate with them, but we don't know their language, and they don't know ours. Do you have any ideas about what they might want?"

Daeira circled the two roaches slowly, and then she reached out her two front pods in friendship. The two roaches didn't reach back, as ants would know to do, but lowered their bodies and spread their front pods out from their sides. She walked around them again as they remained in the lowered position and twitched her antennae, wondering what to do.

At the twitch, the two roaches rose. Daeira lifted her front pods in a questioning gesture and said slowly in Ant, "What do you want?"

The larger of the two pointed to himself and said, "Sir Rainart." Then he gestured to the other roach and said, "Rashad."

Daeira pointed to herself and said, "Daeira."

The two nodded, lowered themselves again briefly, and repeated the name. Daeira pointed to the ground, grass, and the sky, saying the words in Ant. The roach named Rashad repeated each word she said. Rainart remained quiet.

Daeira turned to Delana. "I think they want to learn our language so we can communicate. But I feel something else, too; I don't understand it yet."

Delana nodded but remained silent. Daeira stared at the two roaches and lifted up a thought, Essence, are they to be trusted? No words from Essence came into Daeira's mind, only a mixed feeling: maybe yes, maybe no.

The silence continued.

Finally the smaller roach lowered himself, spread out his front pods again and said, "Daeira, chenche Rashad sky, ground, grass, chenche, chenche."

Daeira had never felt so conflicted before. It was now clear to her that the roaches wanted to learn the Ant language, but the feeling of warning remained. Would teaching them bring on the sorrow she had dreamed about? Or would teaching this roach prevent the predicted trouble? Why couldn't Essence be as clear about this as she had about the dream?

Daeira rubbed her head with one front pod and walked around the two roaches again, trying to see whether she felt an air of goodness about them, as she always felt when greeting a colony member. The two lowered themselves, but then Rashad rose and extended his two front pods. He understood the greeting! He did want to learn. Daeira reached out and touchd his pods with hers. Again, the feeling she got was neither good, nor bad—just different.

A soft breeze brought a fresh, earthy smell and the sound of grasshoppers clicking their mandibles as they chomped the lush grass. Daeira made a decision. "Delana, I feel certain they want to learn our language. I don't know whether their purpose is good or not, but it would be wise to be able to talk to them either way."

"Will you be able to teach them with all your other duties?"

"Yes, I think I can. And as they follow me around and listen, they will learn our ways as well. That may be a very good thing."

The other ants standing by, including the messenger, drifted away to their regular tasks now that there did not seem to be any immediate danger. Only Daeira and Delana remained with the two roaches. "Come," Daeira said, motioning with her right front pod that they should follow her, "I will teach you to speak Ant."

Sir Rainart gestured to Rashad that he should follow. Then he pointed to himself and looked back to the way he had come. He said something to Rashad that Daeira could not understand. Then he walked away.

Daeira turned again to Rashad and repeated, "Come," as she walked toward the colony entrance.

Rashad followed her.

2.

Sixth Time Frame 5, 294 C.C.I.
(Combined Colonies of Insectia) Henry Roach-Dairier II

To: *Master Daisy, Chief Archivist*
        South Dairy Colony 1
        Combined Colonies of Insectia

From: *Henry Roach-Dairier II*
        Meadow Commonwealth
        Roacheria

Sixth Time Frame 5, 294th Season Cycle C.C.I.

Dear Master Daisy:

I am writing for your permission to come and work in the archives of South Dairy 1 with the goal of completing an account of the Inception of the Combined Colonies in the tradition of my grandfather Henry Roach-Dairier's work. I have been preparing for this task since my grandfather died when I was thirteen season cycles old. I completed my basics at Meadow Commonwealth and then did the traditional three-season-cycle job exploration phase (some here at Meadow Commonwealth, some in New South Dairy 50, and a little around the City of Roacheria) even though I already knew what I wanted for my life's work. When I had free time during job exploration in the City of Roacheria, I checked out and read every volume of Roachstory and literature I could get my pods on. I then traveled to South Harvester 45 and lived with distant relatives of my great-great-grandmother. I completed a mentorship in the art of writing under two different mentors: one who had me report on events and write articles for the

Colony Bulletin and a second who guided me through the research process in South Harvester 45's archives and through a systematic study of Antstory and literature.

I am willing to perform any service needed in exchange for the privilege of having access to any and all records available from the time when the roaches enslaved the colony. I look forward to hearing from you.

> *Sincerely,*
> *Henry Roach-Dairier II*

To: Henry Roach-Dairier II
Meadow Commonwealth
Roacheria
From: Master Daisy, Chief Archivist
South Dairy 1
Combined Colonies of Insectia

Sixth Time Frame 15, 294, C.C.I.

Dear Henry:

Your letter gave me great joy! Your great-great-grandfather and your grandfather did so much for all the colonies. I know your project will mean a great deal to everyone. Please, come as soon as possible. There are guest quarters here at the archives and I will be happy to help you find everything you need. I look forward to meeting and working with you.

> *Sincerely,*
> *Master Daisy*

Sixth or Seventh Time Frames, 22 B.C.C., Exact Dates Unknown

Rashad was a quick learner. Master Daeira used many images and quickly drawn figures to explain Ant words and phrases. Rashad repeated them endlessly. Daeira noticed that he could understand the main point of many conversations when she remembered to speak slowly and in short sentences, but he groped for words when he needed to speak. He was attentive to everything she said and showed her great respect. He observed her mannerisms and copied them when they were in any social situation. In just a few weeks, he and Master Daeira were able to have short conversations in Ant.

"Rashad," Master Daeira asked at the beginning of his second time frame, "the day you came, you said 'chenche'. Does that mean 'teach'?"

Rashad hesitated, and then he said, "Yes. But I am learn your language. No teach you mine."

"Will Rainart come back for you?"

"Yes."

"When?"

Again Rashad hesitated. "Sir Rainart say six time frames."

Six time frames, not quite half a season cycle. Master Daeira rubbed her outer mandibles with one front pod. Then she went back to the large black slate she had borrowed from one of the training centers and reached for her white rock writing tool. "You are very intelligent and quick to learn. You soak up knowledge like an aphid sucking sap, but it will take more than half a season cycle for you to be a truly good interpreter."

His face went blank.

She had forgotten again—letting her words come too fast and her sentence go too long for him to understand it all. "I'm sorry," she said. "Let me say that again."

Daeira took the time to recall and write down exactly what she had said. It took another h-unit to go over the meaning of the more complex sentence and the literary device she had used that he did not understand. It wasn't the first time she had to remind herself that she had to break down everything she said into simple grammatical patterns.

When she completed the lesson, Rashad smiled. "Thank you." He pointed to the words soak up knowledge like an aphid sucking sap, pointed to himself and said, "I like that. You are teacher like good mother."

Daeira smiled in return. "Thank you! It's time for lunch. Shall we go?"

Daeira found that Rashad's understanding continued to improve faster than his speaking. During the next time frame, she concentrated on speaking slowly and tried to get more information out of her trainee.

"The first day you came, you stooped like this," Daeira demonstrated. "I did not know what that meant. I walked around you thinking. I twitched my antennae. You stood up. What did it mean to you when I twitched my antennae?"

Rashad's words came slowly. "We do this," he stooped and spread his front pods to the side, "show respect." He twitched his antennae. "Mean you accept respect."

Daeira smiled. "I did that by accident. What if I had not done that?"

"I stay low."

"I will remember that when Rainart returns for you."

"Now I learn more, please."

Over the next few time frames, Daeira tried to ask him other questions about Roacherian customs and what she should say or do when Rainart came back. All Rashad would say was, "I do not know words. I learn words from you."

Nagging doubts pulled at Daeira. She had not had any more troubling dreams, but she still had strong negative feelings about the other roach, Rainart. "Why did you come to us? Truly."

18

But Rashad only emphasized, "Learn your talk."

"No roach ever wanted to learn before. No one even came close to us."

"We want learn now. We came."

"Why do you want to learn now?"

"I keep say it—learn your talk. Then...do things...together."

When Daeira tried to find out why he had hesitated, Rashad changed the subject. "How grasshoppers grow? They are good eat."

"They are good to eat," she gently corrected. He repeated the grammar pattern. The lessons went on.

Ninth Time Frame
294 C.C.I. Henry Roach-Dairier II

I had been working in South Dairy 1's archives for about three time frames when Master Daisy interrupted me one day. "Henry, there is someone here who wishes to meet you. She has something not even I knew existed."

I wiped the fresh ink from the tip of my pod and put the cork in the ink bottle. "Of course. Who?"

An elderly female entered the chamber and extended both her front pods to me. "I am Darlene. You know that Daeira, like most of our spiritual leaders, chose not to have a mate and family. I am a direct descendent of her sister. This," she held out what was obviously a very old journal, "has been carefully passed down through my family for generations. All Master Daeira's teachings and public writings are housed here in the archives, but she kept a personal journal, too. When I heard you had come here, and what you were planning to write, I began to read it. Even though it is very personal in some places, I think it is important to what you are doing, especially some of the conflicted feelings it seems Master Daeira had. It is yours now."

I took the journal from her hands and immediately felt a great reverence for it. "Surely, you don't mean for me to keep this, just to read it and make notes. It should remain here in the archives when I have finished with it."

Darlene smiled at me. "Perhaps you are correct." She turned to Master Daisy. "Will you keep it here then?"

"I'd be honored!" Master Daisy said, embracing Darlene.

Thus it was that I came upon Master Daeira's inner, and most private, thoughts and fears.

Eleventh Time Frame, 22 B.C.C.

Rashad had carefully kept track of the days he was in the ant colony, marking the end of each time frame. He pointed out the day to Daeira when Sir Rainart would return.

"Tomorrow is day, no wait, is the day, Sir Rainart comes back. I must meet him on the surface at noon. Like the day I came."

"Is it that late in the fall already? The time has gone so fast," Daeira said. "You really must ask him if you may stay with us longer. You have learned a lot, but not enough."

"I know I must learn more. Let me talk to him alone tomorrow."

"All right. I will stay close by, but not close enough to listen." Daeira would not have understood the roaches' conversation anyway, but she recognized their need for privacy. She still wondered why he would not share the meanings of any Roach words with her.

The following day was one of those crisp, clear blue sky days that come after the summer's heat has finally diminished—Daeira's favorite time of the year.

Daeira and Rashad went to the surface a little before noon and sat down at the spot where they had first met. Daeira had explained the situation to Delana, who had instructed those caring for the grasshopper herd to graze the hoppers in a different part of the meadow that day. The spiritual guide kept her promise to sit at a distance when they saw Sir Rainart approach. However, she could not help but notice that the volume of Rainart's voice rose several times in what Daeira interpreted as anger. Each time, Rashad would speak softly and Rainart's voice would drop again. Finally, Sir Rainart got up and stomped off the way he had come.

Rashad came back to where Daeira sat. "Sir Rainart say I may learn from you a full season cycle."

"I'm glad to hear that."

"I think maybe I work in the colony some? You tell me all young adult ants do job…job…"

"Job exploration?"

"Yes, job exploration. I practice talking to many ants that way. Maybe learn better. Understand all ants better, too."

The two of them were near the colony entrance by this time. Daeira stopped and looked into Rashad's eyes, trying to see whether he was sincere about this. He averted his eyes and looked down— another thing he had told her showed his respect—but when he did that, she could not "see" the feeling she hoped to.

"Perhaps that would be a good thing. I will talk to our council right away. You could spend every morning with me and the afternoon at some simple job."

"Yes, I like that. I will help you, too, the way all ants work."

Daeira smiled. She took him back to her work chambers and had him practice writing ant symbols while she went to see Delana. She did not mention to Delana (as they set up a simple schedule of tasks) how the tone of Sir Rainart's voice had bothered her. Nor did she mention that a sense of tightness had come into her thorax again, or how the nagging doubts had returned. She was too unsure of the meaning of these feelings to tell anyone in the colony.

 **3.**

Late Fall, 22 B.C.C. and Winter, 21 B.C.C.

Rashad's interpreting ability increased dramatically when he began to work throughout the colony. He groped less for the words he needed and the ants he worked with understood him more easily. Once he learned that personal questions were considered rude, he always prefaced a question with, "Please, excuse me, I don't want to be rude, but I am trying to learn. Why do you . . .?" asking whatever he wanted to know. Most of the ants he talked to answered his questions. While many others and Master Daeira wanted to ask him more about his life in Roacheria, they refrained, trying to model an example of politeness for him. Ant culture taught that one should wait for someone to open up about himself when he wanted to, and Rashad never offered such information.

In his tenth timeframe with the ants, Rashad asked to work in the plastic mine. "Master Daeira, I have worked with the tunnel cleaners, hauled dirt to the surface, and watched those who take care of aphids and grasshoppers. I really learned a lot from them. I have followed those who take messages around the colony. I think I should work in your plastic mine, too. Would that be all right?"

"I'll check with Delana, but I don't see why not."

The next day, Rashad followed Daeira to one of the middle levels of the south side of the colony where the ants mined their plastic. "Our plastic mine takes up most of this side of the colony," Daeira explained as they moved down a slanted tunnel. "There are many entrances, but this is where most of the current work is being done. Above, where there is no more plastic, the old tunnels have been filled in to keep the whole colony strong. We have not yet found the bottom of the plastic deposits. We will not have to worry about plastic for our young's developing minds for many generations to come."

Rashad nodded. "Will I dig or haul?" he asked.

"Neither. Digging is handled by tunnel engineers who study three or four season cycles to know how to direct the digging so that tunnels do not collapse. Hauling is easier for us to do because we have so much more strength."

Rashad was relieved to hear that, remembering how difficult hauling dirt from recent tunnel and domicile digging had been for him.

"You will probably help sort plastic and plastiglomerate from dirt and other waste."

Rashad stared at her. "Plasiglo…what?"

"Oh, I'm sorry. Plastiglomerate is when bits of plastic have become fused, or stuck to, other materials to form a soft rock that breaks up easily."

"Oh, I can do that."

Rashad always did whatever was asked of him without complaining. But several ants mentioned to Daeira that he seemed to spend any time off poking his antennae around other tunnels, always with the comment, "I was wondering what was down this way. If it was wrong for me to look, I am so sorry."

As the day when Sir Rainart would return for Rashad came closer, he asked to spend less time working and more simply talking to anyone who had time to listen. "I have such a good feeling about all of you," he told Daeira. "I hate to take your time, but I feel there is still a lot I do not know."

"You are very good at our language now. I am amazed by how fast you have learned."

Rashad flipped one front pod. "Well, your language really is easy. It's a good thing I wasn't trying to teach you. Our language is much more complex."

"What comes next for you?"

Rashad slipped one pod casually up and off the tip of one antenna. "I will go back with Sir Rainart when he comes. I will report all I have learned. Then more of us will come to visit you. I will be able to tell you what they want and how we will…work together."

A sudden tight feeling gripped Daeira. "How many more will come?"

"Oh, uh...I don't know. It depends on who is interested...I suppose. Sir Rainart never told me that. Would it matter?"

"Well, we don't have a lot of chambers for guests. Most of our living areas are full of our families."

"Yes, I understand. I have visited many of your domiciles. I will be sure to tell Sir Rainart that perhaps only a few should come."

Fifth Time Frame 28, 21 B.C.C.

Rashad had been with the ants a full thirteen time frames—one season cycle—so the appointed day of Sir Rainart's return had arrived. Rashad said many thanks to Daeira and to those he met as he sauntered up the slanting main tunnel to the surface. "Goodbye for a short time," he said to all, "Thank you for all I have learned. I will return with more visitors soon."

He took Daeira's front pods briefly and said, "I'll head back and meet Sir Rainart along the way. I don't know the exact day, but I will see you again soon."

The moment he was out of sight of the ants, Rashad picked up his pace, clicking his mandibles as he went along. "Sir Rainart, where are you?" he called out.

Sir Rainart stepped out from behind a wood plant. "I'm right here. Invasion forces are waiting, hidden, on the other side of the river."

Rashad immediately stooped and flung his front pods out to the sides. While still in a lowered position, he made a humble request. "Sir, may we speak? I need to explain the best way to do this from what I have learned about the ants."

"Not if it involves anther long delay. I can't wait any longer!"

Sir Rainart's mine had run empty two season cycles ago while he was off using up a large portion of his assets buying the influence he needed to secure the City of Roacheria as the seat of government for South Organized Roacheria, even though it made no practical sense to have government agencies on the far western side of roach-controlled surface rather than at a more central location closer to the Great River. He had kept his employees digging in his mine to keep up the pretense of wealth (and, hopefully, hit another layer of plastic) so that the various cities of South Roacheria would combine—something he and others in power agreed was practical for all concerned. But he was quickly running out of resources. He would lose all his power and credibility if he didn't get his pods on this ant colony's plastic, and quickly, before any other Roacherian mine owners or fellow SRCB members found out he was practically broke.

"No, sir. Not a long delay. Only a few days, but, please, listen. You may not need the expense of your warriors. This colony has vast resources, not just in plastic. I have seen it. But you may not need brute force to take it."

Finally, Sir Rainart tipped his antennae to acknowledge his underling's humility. "You have five moments to explain."

Rashad rose half-way and faced his employer. "Sir, if you listen to my idea, you may be able to take over this colony's plastic mine without shedding any life juice."

Rainart shifted his back pods. "And how will I do that?"

Rashad lowered his eyes and antennae. "They are really simple creatures, Sir. Very concerned with sharing what they have with every colony member—great or small. They make sure that everyone, and especially their young, get sufficient plastic. Everybody works at something! I have worked with them in many areas of the colony. I know my way around! I know every tunnel and level. They are peaceful by nature, but I have seen how those who mind the grasshoppers, even the females, fight off the great mantis and other predators."

"So I need more forces?" Sir Rainart pulled up some spring flowers and threw them down in anger.

"No, no, wait; hear me out. I have put on a great act for the last several time frames, telling them how some of our families struggle to provide enough plastic—and you know that is true. I have gained their sympathy, because they believe so much in having enough plastic for all their young. I told Daeira, the one who taught me, that more will 'visit' and we will 'work together.' Sir, I know what you told me in the beginning, but it doesn't have to be that way. You can take over this colony peacefully!"

"You make no sense! Start making sense or I invade tomorrow morning."

Rashad took a deep breath, wishing he were anywhere on the planet but here. "Daeira said they don't have a lot of extra places for 'visitors.' So, in the beginning, only a few should come and they should actually work in the mines. I'll tell the ants that the reward for the roach workers would be to take their share of plastic, just as the ants do. Those who come, can camp on the surface—at first. That will go smoothly. Trust me! Then a few more, and a few more, and then we have them dig more homes, and more.... Do you see now?"

Rashad stood very still, head and eyes looking down at the ground.

Sir Rainart stroked his mandible with one pod and paced around in thought—trampling the flowers he had thrown down. He mumbled as he paced. "Hmmm, cost of warrior pay, warrior death fee as head of a family...balance against no plastic, or not much, for a while longer...." He looked at the statue-still Rashad. "I'm willing to try this for one time frame. Five workers the first quarter time frame, then ten the second, then ten more the third. If it goes well, we'll keep increasing like that, and you'll get a bonus. If it doesn't, I'll invade in one time frame. Agreed?"

"Agreed, Sir. Will you continue to trust me as I explain this to the ants? Will you promise to keep your voice low? Remember how you grew angry seven time frames ago? Even though Daeira couldn't understand your words and sat in the distance, I could tell she was anxious. She said nothing to me, but I could see it in her eyes. You could gain or lose everything with an angry tone. Her trust in me is very fragile right now. I think she senses things that others are not aware of. That is why she is their spiritual leader. That is why they brought her to us that very first day. You and I must keep them docile. That is the way to take over and manage this colony."

Sir Rainart flung both front pods into the air. This was the gamble of his life. His entire fortune, or what was left of it, was on the line now. The possibility of saving a substantial amount of credit by taking the ant colony without the expense of aggression was very appealing. "As I said: one time frame."

Thirteenth Time Frame, 294 C.C.I., Henry Roach-Dairier II

I had assumed that getting the Roacherian side of this chronicle would be the easy part, because as a Roacherian citizen, and with my mother's position as a board member, I would have access to roachstorical archives. One should never make assumptions in Roacheria, even in these modern times. I gained entrance to the archives with no problem, but very little was there! Had the SRCB (South Roach Control Board—as it was at that time) as a collective body wanted to forget about the whole affair? There was a large gap between the "glory days" we learned in basic training and reports about how those days ended.

I found that portions of some news articles had been cut out. Old Roachstory books actually had pages torn out! Fortunately, I had the names of key roaches involved from South Dairy 1's records. I searched hatching, mating, and death records for descendants of these individuals and current directories to find where they lived. With the research I had already done, I guessed that those of Rainart's family might be the better place to start. My status as a journalist got me an appointment with a middle-aged widow, Rabiah, a direct descendant of Sir Rainart.

An h-unit of deep meditation helped me relax before walking to her home and tapping on the thick and imposing portal of a very old, but well-kept-up mansion. I remembered reading something my great-great-grandmother Henrietta had once written. In her study of the ancient extinct Duo Pods, she had once stated that the homes of wealthy roaches looked like an attempt to rebuild Duo Pod ruins. A servant motioned to me to enter and led me to a parlor. An antique portrait with the name Sir Rainart on the frame hung on one wall. A face to go with what I already knew! I etched it into my memory while waiting for my hostess.

When Rabiah entered, I gave all due respect. She twitched her antennae in response to my stooping and then held out both front pods to me with the words, "I'm a little familiar with the ways you follow. I think this is how you greet others?"

I smiled. "Yes, thank you," I said as I gently touched both her front pods. That she knew about the ways of Antism was a good sign.

"Please, sit down," she said, pointing to one of four soft cushions around a low table.

When both our abdomens rested on the cushions, she looked me straight in the eyes. I lowered my eyes slightly, but kept contact with hers. She held my gaze for a moment before saying, "So what does the grandson of the notable Henry Roach-Dairier want with me?"

"Like my grandfather, I am searching for truth." Then I described my project.

"How would I possibly be of any help in that?"

"I was hoping, because your ancestor Sir Rainart was directly involved, that there might be a journal or letters that might have been passed down through the generations. From what I have already learned, I think that such letters, or a journal, if they did exist, might shed a more positive light on the Roacherian side of that unfortunate time."

Rabiah shifted as though she might be feeling awkward.

"I don't mean to offend you," I tried to reassure her. "The research I've done so far in the Combined Colonies paints, of course, a dark persona for all the roaches. But here and there, I found the slightest hints that Sir Rainart was not nearly the despot that his successor was."

Rabiah shifted again. "What makes you think my roachcestor would have kept a journal?"

"I believe one might have existed because most board members, now and back then, kept journals. Sir Rainart was a key figure among those who eventually brought the cities of South Roacheria together into the earliest form of our present government. Ants often keep journals, too. My grandfather kept one. I keep one, and I've found such journals in both South Harvester 45 and South Dairy 1."

"If there were such a journal, and if it could be found, what would you do with it?"

"I would hope that you would allow me to read it and take notes so that I might present the whole truth."

A servant entered with tea. Rabiah looked directly into my eyes again as she filled two mugs. She offered me one. "What if it turned out, assuming a journal existed and was found, that it made a poor reflection on my roachcestors and our clan? We have suffered many indignities and often been excluded by some 'high society members' on that account."

"If you found such a journal, I assume you would read it first. It would be your choice whether or not to tell me you found it. If a journal is not found, my only option is to present my work entirely from the ant point of view—which would definitely be negative."

A slight smile passed over her mandibles. "Did you study law like your grandfather and your mother?"

"Only a few basic courses. You seem to know a lot about me." I took a sip of my tea.

A soft "humph" escaped from her mandibles. "Did you think I would not check into your background when I received your first letter? I don't admit just anyone into my home."

"A wise thing to do. I must have passed the first test then, or we would not be speaking in such a pleasant way."

"This dwelling has many storage chambers filled with cartons of papers and records. It may take me a good bit of time to find, or not find, what you seek. Please return at this same time and day next quarter time frame. I'll let you know if I have found anything."

"Thank you. I truly appreciate your efforts."

Rabiah nodded.

I finished my tea, rose, and left with her servant, more hopeful than I had been when I entered.

The next quarter time frame I returned. The servant smiled at me this time and led me to the parlor I had been in before. Rabiah was already seated there with a young female beside her. I stooped before both of them.

"No need to bow anymore, Henry," Rabiah said, holding out both front pods. "I would like you to meet my daughter, Raissa. She has been helping me search."

Raissa favored her lovely mother except for a terrible scar across her face and another along her abdomen. I wondered what kind of an accident had caused such injuries, but I didn't want to be rude. I greeted Raissa and lowered my abdomen onto a soft cushion Rabiah pointed out. Raissa gave me the same type of penetrating look her mother had on our first visit. We seemed to be about the same age, so I returned her stare. She broke into a smile.

"Please bring some ale and refreshments," Rabiah said to her servant. Then she turned to me. "We have looked through many cartons, but there are so many more to search through. Don't give up on us, though. Will you please share with us a little of your research so far?"

"Certainly," I replied. We spent an h-unit sipping ale (a step up from tea) and snacking on crisp fried bee's wings while I told her the basics of what I had uncovered. Again, I was asked to return in a quarter time frame.

This pattern continued for a full time frame. By my fourth visit, Rabiah excused herself after her usual greeting and left me in the chamber with Raissa. This surprised me, but I didn't mind. Raissa was delightful, and I saw in her an inner beauty that made me forget the scar on her face. We ended up talking about several topics other than my work. I had to admit I liked being able to talk to a female my age (other than those at Meadow Commonwealth) about literature, music, and art. It made me remember my grandfather's descriptions of visiting his cousin season cycles before.

I found myself looking forward to my next visit—and not just hoping they had found a journal. My fifth and sixth visits went the same way. By this time, I had run out of other research leads. My efforts to contact Sir Rastus, descendant of Sir Ragnar, had resulted in letters returned to me that had been opened and then resealed with "NO" scrawled across them and a portal slammed in my face. I needed to plan a trip to Fire Colony 2 for more information.

Once my travel plans were set, I brought up the subject again. "Raissa, I really enjoy our visits and the time we've spent getting to know each other. But I have to leave Roacheria again for a while. I'll be leaving in a few days to go to Fire Colony 2 to see what is available in their archives. I received a letter from the archivist, and she is anxious to work with me. Have you and your mother made any more progress searching?"

Raissa's face suddenly expressed sadness. "You'll be leaving? Really? When will you be coming back?"

I found myself feeling sad, too. "I'm not sure, but I'll probably be gone several time frames."

Raissa shifted on her cushion and her mandibles moved as if swallowing something. "Please, wait here a minute. Let me get some refreshments."

She rose and left the chamber. She returned quickly, but not with refreshments. She had a tattered book in her pods. "Henry, I have to tell you something, and I'm sorry I've waited so long. I confess; my mother and I found this in the very first carton we opened. But, as you told her that first day, that she would probably want to read it first, and then I wanted to read it, too. And then I just wanted to spend more time with you. Now I'm afraid I'll never get to see you again." For the first time, she pointed to her face. "I don't get many male callers, you see, in spite of my mother's fortune."

Since she had pointed out her scar, I was tempted again to ask about it, but refrained. I had almost stopped seeing it. "Then there are a lot of foolish males in Roacheria who don't know what's really important."

"You are much too kind." She placed the long-hoped-for journal in front of me. "It's yours now."

I had to concentrate to keep my pods from shaking as I picked up the book I had so hoped and believed existed. Now, finally, here it was. The words "thank you" seemed insufficient.

"Raissa, I hardly know what to say. This is amazing …surely you will want it back once I've finished reading and taking notes, so, of course, I'll be coming to see you again."

I wanted to see her again for much more than that. While male/female courtship in Roacheria was not as formal as it had been in my grandfather's youth, I still wondered how accepted I really was. There was a great difference in "rank" between Raissa's family and my own. "Would your mother approve if I…came to see you formally—I mean not just for my work?"

As if from nowhere, Rabiah appeared. "Of course I would approve! Did you really think I wasn't close by all these times?"

My smile could have cracked a mandible. "No, of course not," I blurted out.

Rabiah strode across the chamber and took both my pods in hers. "Henry, I've also read the Roach translations of your grandfather's writing. I would not have invited you back if I hadn't approved of the time you've already spent with my daughter. However, I do appreciate the respect you have shown. Yes, once you finish with this journal, I would like to have it back. But keep it as long as you need it. Take it with you on your journey. I'm sure Raissa would enjoy writing to you while you are away. Will you have a message box where you are going?"

"Yes, but I don't know what it will be yet. I have your address, though. I'll include mine in my first letter."

Rabiah stepped back and turned to leave the chamber. "Oh, and Henry, you have my permission to do more than touch Raissa's pods in greeting, but I am close by."

Before I left that day, I gently embraced Raissa and stroked her antennae once. My heart raced in more ways than one as I carried the journal back to Meadow Commonwealth.

4

Sixth Time Frame 6, 21 B.C.C. (12 O.R.)

Rashad entered the colony alone a few days later. Ants were used to seeing him, so he entered easily with a quick greeting. He went directly to Daeira's chamber and tapped on the portal. When she opened it, he spoke immediately. "Master Daeira, please come with me to the surface. Along the way, I will tell you about a dreadful thing that has happened to some roaches."

"What?" Daeira asked.

"A terrible time for some of our workers. Please, just come with me."

As they walked along the tunnel to the surface, Rashad poured out a tale of woe. "One of our plastic mines, the one owned by my employer, Sir Rainart, has run dry of plastic. This means our workers have no more work. Your system, where you just send workers to some other area, is not like ours. Under our law, these workers will get no more credit—they can't buy plastic for their young! Those young will suffer from a lack of plastic. Do you know how awful that is?"

"Yes, sometimes things happen accidentally to our pupating young and they don't receive necessary plastic nourishment. In the most severe cases, they emerge from pupation unable to learn anything."

"So you understand how terrible it is for these families then?"

When they had reached the surface and were a short distance from the main entrance, Daeira asked, "Don't your officials see the need of these families and provide for them?"

"No, sadly, in our society, we are all on our own. That is why I came to you—or why Sir Rainart asked me to come to you. He …is saddened that he had to let some of his workers go. Since I was able to work in your mine, doing the sorting, he wondered if these five workers might not be able to work for the colony. They will camp here on the surface, not live in the colony, of course. Then they could take the plastic they had earned by their work to their families and their young ones—just like I went to your markets for the things I needed while I worked with and learned from you."

At just that moment, Sir Rainart and five male roaches stepped from behind some bushes that grew near the colony entrance. Sir Rainart stopped and spread his front pods to the sides. The five workers were very thin and small, and their exoskeletons were dull, compared to Sir Rainart and Rashad's, whose dark brown shells glistened in the sun. The five males prostrated themselves on the ground.

Taken aback, Daeira quickly tipped her antennae. Sir Rainart stood, but the others remained prostrate. "I can't say 'yes' on my own; I must ask our council."

"Yes, of course," Rashad said. "May we wait here?" Then he spoke softly in Roach to Sir Rainart and the others. Sir Rainart nodded.

Half an h-unit later, Daeira returned to the surface with Delana and three other council members. Rashad hurried to whisper something to Sir Rainart, who showed the council chief and members his respect.

Daeira spoke. "I have explained your request to Delana. She and these council members, who speak for the rest of the council, agree that out of compassion for your young, these five may work in our mine temporarily."

Rashad was noticeably relieved. "Thank, you; thank you!" Then he spoke rapidly to the roaches. Daeira heard him say, "Thank you," in Ant several times.

Sir Rainart repeated the Ant word awkwardly, but with respect. The five males mumbled something unintelligible but seemed to be trying to express gratitude.

"I will remain with them, of course, to teach them as you taught me, and to make sure they…behave appropriately," Rashad said.

Sixth Time Frame 13, 21 B.C.C.

Seven days later, another group of five male roaches appeared, asking for Rashad. Behind them, stood the families of the first group, five females, each carrying a bundle of "furnishings" and followed by several nymphs. Two of the females carried cage-like contraptions with very tiny nymphs inside them. Sir Rainart was not with them. Once again, Daeira went with Rashad. Delana and some of the council members came when called for.

It was quite a reunion of the first five males and their families. Females fell down at the feet of their respective males. Middle-sized nymphs covered their fathers with embraces. The males smiled and said, "Thank you," several times to the ants—pronounced correctly this time.

"You see how wonderful it is what you have done," Rashad said. "But here are five more males who now need work as desperately as the first ones. Is it possible…? Things have gone so well these last few days. You see how willing they are to work…."

The ants admitted the additional group of five male workers.

However, they were not expecting the families of the first group to stay and set up housekeeping in the "camp"—if one could call it that—of roach workers. This camp had been hastily set up each evening once the roach workers finished their tasks in the ant plastic mine. It consisted of one shelter, of sorts, made of fallen branches covered with grass, where all the males had slept; a collection of rusted pots with which they had cooked over an open fire; and bowls they had eaten from.

Rashad was reassuring to his hosts. "That is where the females will be most helpful. They will clean this mess up in no time and put up some better…uh…shelters."

Delana, Daeira, and the other council members looked at the pathetic group and nodded their antennae. A few h-units later, other ant workers were helping put together dwellings made of soil and rock from recent tunnel digging mixed with water and "soil stiffener" that the sun would dry into a firm clay-like substance. The female roaches followed gestured directions and really were good helpers. Each shelter was a hollow half-sphere with an opening on one side. These dwellings would keep out all but the worst rains.

Once completed, the female roaches repeated their gestures of respect over and over, backing slowly into their "homes" with the bundles they had carried, and calling to their nymphs (who had been climbing all over everything) to come inside.

Work proceeded around the colony. The roaches did indeed work hard, showed respect to all the ants and generally stayed out of their way except in the plastic mine. They could not lift the same heavy burdens the ants did with ease, but they made up for it by moving twice as fast with whatever lighter burdens they were asked to carry. The females made their camp as neat as possible and kept control of their nymphs, more or less.

Sixth Time Frame, 21st, 21 B.C.C.

Daeira looked with alarm at the group that arrived the Sixthday after that—families of the second group and ten more males!

"Delana, what should we do? I feel for these creatures. My heart tells me we should help if we possibly can."

"Do you suppose the 'Great Sorrow' you told us about before Rashad arrived was not for us, but for these roach families? Perhaps we are meant to help, and that was the true message Essence sent you."

Daeira closed her eyes for several moments. "Essence has been very quiet for some time. My nights have been dreamless. But sometimes I feel that She expects me to figure things out for myself. Some of the roaches seem very interested in our ways."

"Then this group, also, is welcome," Delana said.

By the end of the first time frame, the roach workers numbered forty, most with mates and nymphs, so that the roach camp now had thirty-something half-sphere mud huts (sometimes two or three single males lived in the same hut with a family) with a total population around 100, including nymphs. Although concerned, Daeira and Delana noticed that the female roaches did keep the surface camp neat and did everything they could to keep their nymphs out of the ants' way. They did not ask for anything, but the ants, because it was their nature, began giving them food.

Rashad was so busy interpreting that Daeira rarely saw him. She summoned him to her chambers the following Fifthday because new batches of roaches had arrived each Sixthday.

She offered her pods in greeting, but her voice had a sternness to it she had never used with him before. "Rashad, even though you came here to learn from us, and I do not wish to be rude with personal questions, there are some things I must ask you."

Rashad went back to his old practice of lowering himself and sweeping his front pods out to the sides, even though Daeira had told him numerous times that it was not necessary. "What is wrong, Master Daeira? Are my fellow workers not doing the right things?"

"No, they are fine. When the first families arrived, I noticed that two of the smallest young were in a cage. That seemed very strange to me. Now, I notice many of your young are in such contraptions. Why?"

Rashad sighed in relief. "Oh, is that all? Have you also seen how the older nymphs run all over, sometimes getting into trouble?"

"Yes."

"Well, you see, the littler ones would get in even more trouble because they don't understand how to behave. We grow up very differently from ants. Also, until their second molt, nymphs often get lost, or eat something not good for them. Before we started using the safety cages, many nymphs died of accidental poisoning. The cage protects a nymph until it is old enough to understand such things. Do you not keep your larva in that thing you call a 'coop'?"

Daeira paused in thought. "Yes, but it isn't completely enclosed."

"Your larva can't run about since they have no legs. Nymphs can run from the moment they hatch. Does this seem right to you now?"

"I think so. One other thing—something much more important.

Delana and the council feel that the colony simply cannot support any more roaches. No more are coming, are they?"

Rashad hesitated. "Ah…I do not think so…at least for now… but I will leave this evening to talk to Sir Rainart and tell him of your concerns."

Rashad hurried along what had now become a trail between the ant colony and his employer's empty plastic mine. It was a two-h-unit trip southeast at his fastest run. (It would have been three h-units for an ant.) The last workers who remained in the shacks surrounding the mine pit (which he noted were not as good as what the ants had built of earth and clay) were packing up their belongings. Although tired, Rashad put on a burst of speed toward the mine's administrative center.

Rashad wished he had a mug of fermented honeydew to calm himself, but he didn't, so he settled for a few deep breaths before approaching Sir Rainart's work chamber.

"Rashad, what are you doing here?" the portal clerk asked.

"I must see Sir Rainart immediately."

"Just a moment. I'll announce you."

The portal clerk put his front pod to the wood and knocked lightly: tap, tap…tap, tap, tap…tap, tap.

"Just a moment," was the muffled reply from within.

The portal opened. Sir Rainart stood at full height, looking down at the prostrate Rashad. Finally, he tipped his antennae and motioned Rashad inside with the instruction to leave the portal opened.

"Why are you here? I told you the schedule for worker arrival."

"Sir…things are …going very smoothly, as I said they would, did I not? No deaths, no warriors, and all that we discussed that would cost you more credit?"

"So far."

"Yesterday, Daeira asked me if more were coming. She said the council feels the colony cannot support any more."

"Oh, she did, did she?"

Rashad lowered himself a bit more, almost begging. "You promised me a bonus if this first time frame went well, and it has. I would like to ask you to use that promised bonus to pay the last workers for another time frame. Please, wait one full time frame more before sending them. Let the ants get a little more used to this whole idea before you begin the total takeover."

"Give up your bonus! I shouldn't have let you stay there for a full season cycle. You actually like those three-blobbed creatures, don't you?"

Rashad's antennae twitched uncontrollably. "No, sir, it's not that I 'like' them, but that I understand them and how they live. I don't see much need to shed a lot of life juice unless there is no other way, and I firmly believe what I am proposing will work."

Sir Rainart twanged one outer mandible—a gesture of extreme disrespect and insult.

Totally flat on the floor, Rashad whispered, "But, sir, it will save you a lot of credit in the long run."

Sir Rainart drummed one front pod on his wooden writing surface. The plastic he had gotten so far was very high quality—better than what his mine had produced at the end. The quantities were not quite up to the amount produced before he hit bottom, but once the rest of the workers were there, it would be the same.

Rashad remained in his position of total submission, wondering whether he was about to be stepped on as punishment for his boldness. It was the first time he had ever realized how soft the floor covering was in Sir Rainart's administrative chamber. He had never paid attention to the pattern of oranges, reds and browns. Having seen such floor coverings in the markets, he knew they cost almost as much as his earnings for half a season cycle.

Finally, Sir Rainart spoke. "Here's how it will be: On the last day of this new time frame, I will have all my warriors camped near the river and ready to invade. I'll send my last thirty workers and their families like I have before. If those ants hesitate at all to accept them, you take that Dae...Die...whatever her name is, up to the top of that wood plant and let her see what she'll get if she says 'No'!"

5

Seventh Time Frame, 21 B.C.C.

The second time frame that the roaches worked in the ant colony and lived in their surface camp went as smoothly as the first. The workers did everything asked of them and behaved in a way that showed respect for authority and appreciation for what they were given. They were, after all, quite used to being told what to do and receiving little in return. In many respects they were better off in the ant colony than they had been in Sir Rainart's mining camp. Daeira and the council chief began to think more and more that this help given to the roaches was what Essence had intended when She told Daeira that a time of sorrow was coming and that the ants needed to pull together in their beliefs.

Only the language barrier prevented friendships from forming between the roach workers and their ant hosts. Neither Daeira, nor any of the other ants, had time to teach them to speak Ant. Rashad had no time either.

When Daeira asked whether she should put out a call for volunteer trainers and arrange some evening sessions for those who might want to learn Ant, Rashad said, "This is to be temporary, is it not? What need have they to learn to speak to you? That is my job."

Summer Solstice arrived. This had always been a festival time in dairying colonies. They were half way through a season cycle, the 14th day of Seventh Time Frame. New grasshopper nymphs that had often jumped wildly away now stayed with the herd, so fewer were lost to predation. The herds began to grow fat on lush summer vegetation. Aphids were at the peak of honey dew production, so the ants began to store more and more in clay vats for winter. In the midst of the hectic activity, the ants paused for a day to celebrate the abundance of nature given to them by Essence.

Several whole grasshoppers were roasting over pits of hot coals on the surface—very close to where the roach families camped. The aroma floated all around. It seemed only polite to invite the roaches to partake in the feast.

Daeira walked over to the roach camp and called out for Rashad. He came quickly. "Rashad, we would like to invite your group to join in our Summer Solstice Feast. Can you explain to them, as I told you once, what this celebration signifies?"

"Thank you, Master Daeira. That is very generous of you. I will tell them what I can about the deep care of Essence in providing a beautiful and bountiful planet. So you desire to celebrate while respecting the balance in nature. Am I remembering that correctly?"

"Yes, your memory always has been excellent."

Rashad called a quick assembly of the roach workers and their families. He thought back to the previous summer when he had been with the ants only a short time. He had thoroughly enjoyed his first Summer Solstice, but it was a delicate game he was playing here. He worried about what the ants would think if they saw some of these roaches after they had consumed a few mugs of anything that had been fermented. A roach celebration typically involved drinking far too much ale.

When the workers had gathered, Rashad climbed to the top of one of the huts so his voice could be heard by all. Daeira, of course, did not know the meaning of the words Rashad spoke that day. He wanted her to think that the loud volume of his voice was so everyone could hear. "Listen, everybody. The ants have invited you to their Summer Solstice Festival. You are going to get a meal that you did not earn and could not possibly buy on the credit Sir Rainart pays you, so be grateful. Behave yourselves and don't act like gluttons! No more than one mug of their fermented honeydew. If anybody takes more, or gets drunk, I'll tell Sir Rainart and you'll find yourselves out of work and on your way back to Roacheria with nothing—and faster than you can lower yourselves to be stepped on."

It was indeed a wonderful celebration. Ant and roach alike had plenty to eat. When a few roaches tried to get a second mug of fermented honey dew, a quick glare from Rashad sent them back to their group. A few of the roaches even tried to mimic the dance steps of the ants as they watched. Ant voices rose in a song of praise accompanied by pea pod shakers and the haunting but joyful notes of breath blown across the tops of hollow reeds of varying lengths.

Rashad went over to Daeira at one point. "Master Daeira, I saw something this evening that I didn't notice last summer. May I ask you a question that might be personal?"

Daeira set her mug on a nearby surface. "You may ask, but if it is too personal, I won't answer."

"I see mated pairs whom I know from working in the mine. But this afternoon, one of each seems to be here at a time. They are not together for this festival. But other mated pairs are here together. Why is that?"

Daeira smiled. "I suppose that never came up before. Too much sunlight is dangerous for our larvae. When a mated pair has a larva, one of them must stay underground with their young one. For other pairs, their young are now pupating, or they are newly mated and the first egg has not hatched yet, so there is no need for one to stay underground."

"Oh, I see. But why is the sun dangerous to larvae?"

"Because larvae have no exoskeleton, heat and light can dehydrate them, causing much suffering and even death. Your roach nymphs don't seem to have that problem since they don't hatch as larva like ours do."

"Thank you for explaining that. Please, excuse me now."

Song and dance continued through the lengthened twilight, but the festival ended when darkness set in. Another workday would follow in the morning.

Rashad made another trip back to Roacheria two days later. He appeared before his powerful employer as humbly as ever.

"I'm sure they will accept your terms," he said at the end of his report.

"What makes you so certain this time?" Sir Rainart asked as he sipped a mug of ale. He had not offered any refreshments to his loyal employee. But Rashad had prepared himself for this meeting. He had carried a jug of fermented honeydew with him and guzzled it just before he arrived. He had not consumed enough to be impaired, but its effect made him feel much more confident than the last time he had been in this chamber.

"Because I know exactly the right threat. I learned something new a few days ago at Summer Solstice."

"And that is?"

"It has to do with their larvae, but don't worry about it. If your warriors are not needed, and you save all that credit, may I make one final request?"

Sir Rainart shifted his abdomen on the soft cushion behind his polished wooden work surface. "You may ask, but I might not grant it."

"You don't have to pay the ants anything for their work, right?"

"Correct."

"And they provide all their food and other needs, and it doesn't cost you anything. You'll soon be getting more plastic out of their mine than yours was producing at the end, so you will be getting back the investment you made in me and this past season cycle, correct?"

More than a hint of irritation was in Sir Rainart's voice. "How would you know what my mine was producing?"

Rashad lowered himself again. "I don't, sir; I didn't, ever. I just noticed that there didn't seem to be much when you first hired me, and a lot is being carted to you now."

"Make your point, Rashad!" Sir Rainart blurted out, now worried about what else his overly-observant employee had noticed.

"When your takeover is complete, please, continue to let the ants have the plastic they need for their young."

"Why should I do that?"

Rashad looked around his employer's work chamber, its walls covered by luxurious woven wall hangings. The colors in the weaving reminded him of the sunset and twilight of that recent Summer Solstice. The thought went through his mind that Sir Rainart was right. That made him wonder why he was risking his own exoskeleton for the ants. But something made him press on with his point.

"Because it will be less expensive in the long run," he said. "If the ants do not get plastic for their young, the old will die off with no workers to replace them. The next generation of your family will end up paying roach workers to do the work the ants would be doing for free."

"You've become quite the economist, haven't you?" Rainart's sarcastic tone was not lost on Rashad.

"No, sir: I wouldn't dare to call myself that. It just seems to make sense to me."

"I do like a cheap labor force. If all goes well, you may continue to allow the ants to draw their shares of plastic." Rainart did not show it, but he realized that, once again, Rashad was saving him credit. This gamble looked like it really could work.

Rashad did not smile as he backed slowly away from Sir Rainart, but he was glad of the assurance he had received. He could continue to walk this narrow line between the ants and his powerful employer. If anyone had asked him why just then, he would have thrown up his front pods in confusion.

Fifth Time Frame, 295 C.C.I. (327 O.R.)
Henry Roach-Dairier II

It was while I was completing my research in Fire Colony 2 that Master Daisy arrived as a visitor.

"Master Daisy, whatever brings you here?" I asked, moving my ink pot aside so she could rest her front pods on the table. I shifted my abdomen to make room for her on the bench.

"You'll never believe what we found. After you completed your research with us, our council decided that perhaps it was time to re-excavate the upper section of the colony where the roach warriors had lived."

I remembered reading the account that when the colony had been liberated, those tunnels had been filled in with soil from new digging—a way of burying all the season cycles of sorrow. Filling in those tunnels had also helped the ants work off accumulated anger. When I was there, a memorial plaque had hung on the tunnel wall covering the filled-in entrance to what had been the roach section.

"Anyway," Master Daisy continued, "a team of archeologists has worked with our tunnel engineers and begun opening it up as a museum. It seemed strange to us that while the tunnels had been filled in, the individual domiciles and the warrior dorms had not collapsed from lack of maintenance. The very first domicile must have been where the interpreter lived. It was dusty and mildewed, of course, but otherwise in perfect condition. You know the accounts of how they found Rashad was gone, but this was sitting right on the eating surface. Why it was left there, and not noticed before, no one knows. The parchment is in amazingly good condition."

Daisy reached into her satchel and withdrew a parcel wrapped in undyed fabric. She opened it to reveal a slightly tattered, but well-preserved pile of parchment. "I don't read Roach, but I think it might be a journal."

"I've been thinking a lot about Rashad lately," I said. "He was quite an enigma."

I looked at the first few pages. The ink was fading, but it was readable in spite of all the season cycles. "Essence be praised! It is a journal!"

As I read through the pages over the next several days, knowing I had a huge copying job in order to preserve it, I knew I would need to revise some of what I had already written and rethink my presentation of what had happened.

6.

Ninth Time Frame, 21 B.C.C.

Rashad dragged his pods on the way to Daeira's chamber very early in the morning after his discussion with Sir Rainart. He wasn't looking forward to what he had to tell her and Delana that day, but it had to be done, and if it didn't go well…he didn't want to think about that.

He tapped gently on the portal. It was obvious from her face that Daeira was not happy to see him. There was an awkward moment of silence.

"Uh, hum, Master Daeira, please come with me. And Council Chief Delana must come, too."

"Let me guess," Daeira said, using a highly unusual tone of sarcasm for an ant. "You want to ask us to accept more workers." She followed him down the tunnel to Delana's domicile—for it was too early in the morning for her to have left home to go to the Council Chamber.

Rashad kept moving down the tunnel. "You will see."

When the three of them reached the surface, Rashad pointed to a tall wood plant, a conifer, growing near the roach family camp. "Please, climb this with me. I must show you something in the distance."

The two female ants gave each other a quizzical look and climbed up behind him.

Once they reached the highest branch upon which they could safely stand, they looked out over the meadows that surrounded the ant colony. The grasshopper herds grazed peacefully off to the left. Over to the right, the aphids sucked sap quietly from the thinner branches of a grove of leafy wood plants. About a quarter d-unit in front of them stood a group of roach workers and families—not a surprise. Beyond them, the familiar river meandered peacefully across the land.

Then they saw what Rashad intended them to see.

On the opposite side of the river, the fiercest roach warriors imaginable stood rank upon rank. By the number of lines and ranks, there were at least half as many as the number of adults in the entire colony—for theirs was not a large colony.

"Rashad…" Daeira's voice wavered.

But before she could say anything more, Rashad spoke in a commanding voice neither of the two females had ever heard before. "Everything will be different from now on. I do not ask you; I tell you what Sir Rainart orders me to say to you. The families you see there are coming to live and work here. From now on, your whole colony works for and belongs to Sir Rainart. You will do what he says, or those ranks of warriors you see will charge through the colony, killing anyone who stands in their way. They will take your larvae out to the surface and leave them in the sun to wither."

Shocked, Daeira and Delana's mandibles opened wide. Delana nearly lost her grip on the branch of the wood plant.

Rashad continued. "But, if you submit to his control, you will live and he will still allow you to keep your current ration of plastic for your young, ensuring their and your future."

A thousand realizations hit Daeira like the force of a severe summer storm. She could barely find words as tears began streaming from her eyes, dripping from her still-opened outer mandibles. "All this time…everything you said…it was all a lie! You betrayed everything I taught you!"

No one said anything for a full moment.

Then Rashad spoke quietly. "I did not betray 'everything'. If you had not taught me, he would have sent his warriors with no choice last season cycle." Then he added with the new firmness, "You have to gather the rest of the council and colony members. You have to tell them how it will be now. You have one h-unit to return here and tell me what your colony chooses: death or life."

Rashad took two colored cloths from his satchel. "If you choose to be controlled by Sir Rainart, I will flash this green pennant. The families will come and the warriors will stay where they are. Or I will flash this red one and the warriors will come."

Daeira and Delana climbed silently down the wood plant's trunk.

"Delana," Daeira said when they reached the ground, "I am the one who advised you to allow Rashad to stay with us last season cycle. I am responsible for all this. I am no longer fit to speak for Essence in this colony. I greatly misinterpreted Her voice. I have brought this great sorrow upon us, not prevented it. Do with me what you will."

Delana shook her head and wiped away a tear with her front pod from where it had dripped onto her mandible. "No, Master Daeira. You heard what Rashad said—that if we had not received him, we would have been attacked from the start. You have given us a chance. We will do what we must, and with Essence, we will live."

The colony had long had in place a procedure for emergency communications. Council Chief Delana spoke only two words to the entrance sentry, "Emergency Message."

Within ten moments, the rest of the colony council and 100 key ants from various parts of the colony (who would take the message to other groups, and on from there until every member had heard) assembled before Delana. They looked anxiously at their Council Chief.

"The Great Sorrow that Essence told Master Daeira about in a dream over a season cycle ago has come upon us." Then she told them about the warriors and how they would now be slaves to the roaches. "But Daeira's work with the roach, Rashad, has helped lessen the blow. Every family will still receive its share of plastic."

The two females answered what questions they could in the short time they had. There was no doubt about the "choice" they had to make. They knew the colony did not have the resources at hand, and on such short notice, for an adequate defense.

With a heart full of sorrow, Council Chief Delana climbed back up the conifer and told Rashad, "Flash the green pennant."

The slavery, or "management" as the roaches referred to it, of South Dairy Colony 1 had begun: Day 6 of Ninth Time Frame, 19 B.C.C. (12 O.R.)

7.

Twelfth Time Frame, 21 B.C.C.

Once they were over the initial shock, the ants found that their lives were not a whole lot different than they had been before. They worked as they always had; they trained their young adults in reading, writing, and other basics and mentored them for tasks around the colony. Young adults found members of the opposite sex they cherished and joined in mating. New young hatched and life went on.

At the beginning of Twelfth Time Frame, Rashad went to Delana. He didn't bother to address her by name or as Council Chief. "It will soon be too cold on the surface. You must find homes for all the families within the warmth of the colony."

Delana twitched her antennae in a formal assent and then added. "It will take some time for us to excavate that many new domiciles."

"Have it done within a time frame," he said. As he reached the portal, he added, "Oh, and make one area a large dormitory for warriors. Some will be coming to keep the peace."

Delana sent messages to Master Daeira and to the colony's tunnel and domicile construction experts. When they had gathered in the council chamber, she said simply, "They want to move underground because of the coming winter rains and cold. Worse, some warriors will begin to live here as well, to 'keep the peace,' as Rashad put it."

A collective sigh rose from the assembled group.

The colony's chief tunnel engineer asked, "How many of them are there now?"

Delana sighed. "I've lost track. Just start excavating somewhere and I'll find out for sure. Rashad says we have only a time frame to complete this."

"One time frame!" the master domicile builder shouted. "I'll need to borrow a lot of workers from other areas."

The babble of voices rose as the ants let out their anger at this new demand. Then they settled down to brainstorm how to accomplish the nearly impossible task. The grasshopper herds could be moved underground a little earlier than usual for the season—the aphids, too. It took fewer workers to manage them underground, which would free up some colony members to help haul dirt from new excavations. Roaches could do all of the plastic mining except for the tunnel digging. That would free up a lot more workers. The domicile and tunnel engineers could divide into two groups and work day and night, extending their time to twelve h-unit shifts. The furnishings the roaches already had would have to do. They simply couldn't give them everything.

The head domicile engineer asked the question they had all been avoiding. "How many warriors must we accommodate?"

Delana hung her head. "He didn't say. I'll find out. If possible, I'll tell him furnishings are out of the question. Master Daeira, will you come with me to ask that? He still looks at you with a small measure of respect. Maybe he'll be a bit more accommodating if you are there."

Daeira nodded. "May I have some time to meditate first? I'm sorry, but I can barely stand the sight of him lately without the calm that meditation brings."

"Of course."

"One other thing," the chief tunnel engineer said. "Where shall we do all this?"

Delana turned toward the council members and raised her front pods in a questioning manner. Quiet reigned for several moments.

Finally, the chief domicile engineer said, "I don't know about the rest of you, but I can't abide the thought of spreading them around the colony. I'd prefer a totally new and separate section for them. What about the north side of the main entrance? It would take us under the grasshopper pasture, but I don't see a problem with that. We can heap up the diggings on that side of the mound for added strength above it, and since we are bringing the herds underground earlier, they won't be trampling that area."

Everyone twitched his or her antennae in agreement. With the plan accepted, the ants went to work.

Rashad stopped scolding one of the mine workers when he saw Daeira and Delana turn the corner of a new tunnel in the mine. He stood as tall as he could to convey his authority.

"May we have a moment of your time, please?" Daeira asked.

"What?" He turned to the roach worker and shooed him back to his task.

"Rashad, we need to know exactly how many domiciles you must have. Also, how many warriors are coming? How much space should their dormitory have?"

Rashad rubbed his outer mandible with one front pod. "There are fifty families now and some unattached workers—but they can each live with a family as they have been. I'll need my own domicile. So that's fifty-one domiciles. You don't need to make them any larger than those you have. Is a chamber two times the size of the Council Chamber possible?" He avoided telling them how many warriors would be coming.

"I'll have to consult our chief domicile engineer. That would be an unusually large chamber. It would have to have some support pillars," Delana said, "and that takes more time."

"I understand. If it can't be that big, just dig two chambers each the size of the Council Chamber. That will accommodate the warriors. Anything else?"

Daeira hesitated. "Rashad...do you remember all that I taught you? It is simply not possible for us to furnish that many new homes in such a short time. The furnishings they own now will have to do."

For a fraction of a second, Rashad lowered his antennae. Then he looked directly at Master Daeira and said, "The workers know they must pay for their furnishings with extra labor. Warriors are accustomed to carrying everything they own in a sack, and they use the sack to sleep in. They won't need anything else except for food, of course."

Daeira returned Rashad's steady gaze. "Thank you."

The two females left to spread the word that more changes would be coming to their colony.

Last Day, the day after Thirteenth Time Frame 28, 21 B.C.C.

Forlorn groups of ants gathered in the colony's largest meditation chamber throughout Last Day for the Winter Solstice the rededication ceremony passed down from one generation to the next. Since everyone wanted to hear Master Daeira's annual message, several services had been scheduled throughout the day. Families signed up for one time or another to keep the numbers balanced and planned their family celebrations around those times.

Master Daeira had spent a sleepless night deep in meditation asking Essence to send her words of hope for the colony. She wrote down what she felt she heard from Essence so she would give the same message to each group.

The previous year, they had sung a song of praise to begin their rededication, but it didn't seem as though anyone was much in a mood to sing, so Daeira had decided to skip that part of the service.

Antstorical note: The songs that later became traditional, and which are still in use, were not written until after the Combined Colonies of Insectia formed. Henry Roach-Dairier II

As the first group of ants to gather settled their abdomens onto the rows of benches, Daeira saw Rashad enter the chamber and stand at the very back. Oh, how she wanted to tell him he was not welcome in this assembly, but she knew she couldn't. Another part of her still hoped that what she had to say would spark a flame of compassion inside his thick exoskeleton. She wanted to believe he would turn from his selfish ways and perhaps convince other roaches to do the same.

First they chanted their creed: "On this Last Day, as we link one solar season cycle to the next and unite it with the thirteen lunar time frames, we remember that all things are linked to each other.

"Essence, Creator of the Universe, and all its cycles, and infinite variety of living things, we offer up our thoughts and dedicate ourselves once again to all that we believe.

"To us has been given the gift of knowledge and the wisdom to discern right from wrong. May we reach out to help each other carry the responsibility of this gift.

"We pledge to respect all living things and the delicate balance of the chain of life; to take care of the planet and seek full understanding of its many cycles; to take no more than we need; to replenish what we take and reuse what we have; to cherish our mates and families and care for each member of our colony, placing the needs and good of others above our own.

"Help us to meditate upon how well we have lived this creed; to seek pardon of anyone we may have offended; to generously forgive all who may have offended us; and to resolve to live the new season cycle even more fully. So be it."

Two beeswax lamps were lit, symbolic of the increase in daylight as each new season cycle began. They provided a dim glow in what had been a totally dark chamber.

Master Daeira then stood before them and spoke:

"My fellow colony members, I sense more changes in our lives will come. It will not be easy for any of us to bear. I know it will be more difficult than I ever imagined when Essence first gave me the vision. Yet, as I recited our creed with you a few moments ago, I was reminded once again that Essence never promised us that life would always be easy. Our creed is a very great challenge, especially now that we are called upon to share our resources with those who would take without asking and demand without consulting. Essence has provided a word for this, since we have never known of it before now. The word is 'steal': to take without asking."

She paused a moment to try to see Rashad's reaction; his face looked like stone.

"It would be easy these days to let our inner essences be turned from cherishing to hating. It would be easy to abandon our most precious values, but that is exactly why we must cling to what we believe all the more. Essence never promised us lives filled with perfection. But she did promise to be with us in our thoughts and dreams. While these days seem dark as a storm at night where there is no light from stars or moon, we must remember that light increases with each new day from here on until Summer Solstice. Our lives move in a cyclical pattern from good times, through difficult days and back to good again, just as sun increases the length of our days and then decreases them again."

Rashad was now looking directly at Daeira.

"My friends and colony family before me," she continued, "even though I do not know how much longer this time of sorrow will be, I feel deep within me, through the depths of Essence, that no matter how many season cycles may come and go, days of light, joy, and good will return. Essence has promised me this, and I pass Her promise on to you. Now as we enter our time of silent meditation, let us ponder the ways we may best support each other."

The ants remained silent, each one lost in his or her uplifted thoughts for nearly half an h-unit. During that time, additional beeswax lamps were lit, gradually bathing the chamber and its occupants in their soft glow.

"As the daylight increases, so does our resolve to live our lives in simplicity and charity," the group chanted.

Daeira saw Rashad leave the chamber. She was grateful that he left before the sharing of honeydew, for she had a feeling that no one would have wanted to offer their mug to him. She would have had to make the effort.

Several ants stepped forward to ladle honeydew from a huge vat into large mugs, which then were poured into the smaller ones for each family attending. When all were served, they raised their mugs and chanted, "Sweet honeydew, gift of the aphid and Essence, fill our lives with Your joy that we may share it with others."

The drinking of honeydew complete, family members embraced each other, stroking the backs of thoraxes and antennae, before they turned to embrace those near them. The silence of meditation was broken by the beginning of cheerful conversations, as all left the meditation chamber to go to their homes.

Eighth Time Frame, 295 C.C.I. Henry Roach-Dairier II

This seems an appropriate time to note that before the Combined Colonies, each ant variety had its own particular Last Day traditions. Harvester ants broke and shared seeds; fire ants carved up roasted beetle or other wild insects they hunted; dairying ants sipped honeydew as described; red dessert ants shared a bread made with ground up cactus; carpenter ants consumed their paste-like wood mixture, etc.

After the Combined Colonies formed, the seed-breaking of the harvesters was chosen to symbolize the sharing, growth (both spiritual and physical), and caring that all ants held precious in their beliefs. As I delved more into the individual traditions of those days, I found that all the colonies, even when there was no communication between them, had remarkably similar words in their creeds. Very few changes were made when the colonies came together so that all said the same words. Everything that had to do with core beliefs, individual colony law, and tradition received only a little revision. Perhaps this is not so remarkable when one considers that ants always had a close relationship with Essence. Every colony had its spiritual leader like Master Daeira. Essence spoke to them on these topics, and when the time was right, She brought them all together in response that period of slavery.

This harmony was in direct contrast to the numerous arguments and political deals, and a few rare compromises, which took place when East and South Roacheria agreed to come under one South East Roach Control Board about ninety season cycles later. The same type of political buy-outs had brought the individual city-states of South Roacheria together in the early days of South Roacheria. The cost of paying for such agreements was what led Sir Rainart to take over his neighboring ant colony in order to preserve his wealth and influence.

_8._

_20 B.C.C._

The roach workers and their families had moved into their section of underground homes about half a time frame before Last Day that season cycle. That was fortunate for them because major rainstorms two days later washed away the domed huts they had been living in. A garrison of 200 warriors arrived on the second day of the new season cycle and occupied the two large dormitories the ants had excavated. The chambers were overcrowded, but the warriors did not complain. The ants feared them because the warrior roaches were over three times the size of the average dairying ant and their mandibles were proportionately larger as well. Ants had to press themselves against some of the smallest tunnel walls when the warriors moved through them. Rashad demanded that the height and width of many tunnels be increased.

The first full year of slavery in South Dairy Colony 1 passed with no major incidents. Rashad kept the roach workers and their families in line and the garrison of warriors minded their own business because there were no problems necessitating their interference. The warriors even kept the mighty mantis and other predators at bay. This was mainly because they had developed a taste for roasted grasshopper and knew when more hopper nymphs survived, there was more meat for everybody. However, the speed at which they could run and drive off a mantis made the ants even more fearful for their own lives should they think about trying to escape from the colony to seek the help of other ants.

This was reinforced when the roaches dug a sizable pit and constructed an inward curving fence of metal wire that they brought from Roacheria. The ants who tended the grasshopper herds passed the word around the colony that they had seen the roach warriors catch two mantises alive (a male and a female) and toss them into that pit. To the ants' horror, when it happened that a roach worker grew angry and struck one of the warriors, everyone was called to the surface to witness "Roach Justice." Both the injured warrior and the offending worker were thrown into the pit to be eaten by the mantises.

Rashad announced in Ant: "This is what will happen to anyone who does not do what they are told."

But nothing Rashad could say stopped the mine workers from having a certain amount of comradery as they toiled together underground sorting plastic from soil and then carting the dirt to the top of the mound or some other part of the colony, or loading the carts that rolled plastic back to Roacheria. Rashad couldn't watch every roach and ant every single minute. He did carefully monitor the amount of plastic shipped out and retained in the ant colony for distribution to each adult ant or family.

19 B.C.C.

Sir Rainart arrived for an official visit at Fall Equinox. A nervous Rashad took him on a complete tour.

Sir Rainart entered the Colony Council Chamber expecting to be properly respected. Rashad lowered himself and said to Master Daeira, "You must lower yourself like this."

Master Daeira looked directly at him and said, "I don't care what you do to me; I will not perform that gesture. I have no respect for him."

"Please, Master Daeira, you must."

"No. Toss me to the mantis; then I may join Essence forever."

Colony Council Chief Delana looked at Daeira and remained in her standing position, too.

Sir Rainart glared at Rashad and demanded in Roach, "What is going on?"

Rashad lowered himself even farther and whispered in Roach, "Sir, remember what I told you about these two early on? You do not need to acknowledge them at all right now. Simply ignore their ignorance. You and I know they are below me and I am below you, but humor them at this moment. Things are going very well, are they not?"

Sir Rainart twanged his outer mandibles and left the chamber.

When they reached the mine tunnels, Sir Rainart nodded his approval to the amount of plastic being processed and Rashad's records of distribution. "Take me to your domicile. We must speak in private."

"Of course, Sir." Rashad led the way back up to the roach section of the colony and opened the portal to his living quarters. He was glad he had taken the time to straighten the place up early that morning.

Once the portal had closed behind Sir Rainart, Rashad lowered himself again. Sir Rainart promptly placed a back pod squarely in the middle of Rashad's thorax and stomped down. Rashad winced beneath his punishment but did not cry out. He feared his powerful master might crack his thorax, but Sir Rainart let him up. Rashad remained on the floor of his parlor.

"Let those two females know I will never overlook their arrogance again! Or yours. Get them trained to know I am in charge here. Increase the plastic shipped to me by 10 percent. If the ants don't have enough for their young, they'll just have to mine more. Another thing, I don't like how my workers are becoming too familiar with the ants. I saw several of them smile at each other as they were lugging their loads. That will come to no good. Tell all the roach families to pack up and return to Roacheria next Seventhday. I'll move the higher ranking warriors into those quarters so the dorms are less crowded. And if you were expecting any bonus, forget it. You've let things become way too lax!"

"Yes, Sir."

"Now get up and go to work."

"Yes, Sir."

"And show me which tunnel gets me out of this hole in the ground."

Rashad did as he was told.

Sir Rainart, escorted by his personal body warriors, spoke briefly to the warrior commander and then left the colony.

A Time Frame Later

Sir Rainart stepped into his favorite night entertainment place in the City of Roacheria and looked around for the one he was supposed to meet. The serving roach approached him and stooped low. "Sir, come this way, please. Your party awaits you in a private chamber."

Sir Rainart nodded. The roach rose and led him to a chamber at the back of the establishment.

"Ah, Sir Rainart, so glad you could join me," Sir Ragnar said. "I'd like you to meet the head of my warriors, Rand."

Rand stooped in respect to one above him. Sir Rainart tipped his antennae. The two board members sat down on comfortable cushions placed near a dining surface.

Rand called for the server. "Bring my master and his friend a keg of ale, fried bees' wings, and roasted beetle." The server nodded, stooped, and hurried out.

Rand stood near the portal of the private chamber, his eyes constantly sweeping the main portion of the establishment and watching all who entered or left.

When the server brought the keg and mugs, he asked Sir Ragnar, "Sir, would you like a dancer to entertain you?"

"Thank you, but not now. Perhaps after we have concluded our business."

"Very good, Sir."

Sir Rainart sipped his ale and turned to his SRCB colleague. "So, what did you wish to discuss with me outside Board Chambers?"

Sir Ragnar set down his mug. "No need to stride around the wood plants, huh? Fine, I'll be direct. We both know your mine went dry. So, where are you getting all this plastic I see with your mark on it in the trade center?"

Sir Rainart did not trust Sir Ragnar for a single moment since most of Rainart's fortune had gone to buy off those who had supported this rival. "What makes you think my mine has run dry?"

"The fact that your village is deserted. Isn't that enough?"

Historical Note: Twelfth Time Frame 295 C.C.I., Henry Roach-Darier II

For the benefit of ants reading this, a roach mine location supported a small community. All the workers lived near the mine and others joined them setting up little markets, places to socialize and drink ale, and providing basic services. All of it was tightly controlled by the roach who owned the mine. Mine owners rarely lived in these villages, but usually maintained a small living space (complete with a couple of servants to cook meals) for their own use when they needed to see to the business of a mine. This was especially true for Sir Ragnar who had to travel quite a distance from his luxurious domicile in the City of Roacheria to get to his "old" mine. He generally lived at the mine during the work week and went back to his home for Sixth and Seventh days. He also went back to the city for S.R.C.B. meetings, etc. If there were two or more plastic mines in close proximity, a town might develop in the middle of them—or an entire metropolis like the City of Roacheria, which was ringed with numerous mines.

The roasted beetle and fried bees' wings arrived on platters. Sir Rainart ignored the discussion for some time while he partook of the food provided by Sir Ragnar.

"They certainly do have the best bees' wings in all Roacheria here," he said. "I thank you for the privilege of dining with you."

"And I, you," Ragnar replied, though Rainart suspected he didn't mean it.

"So, as I was asking, where are you getting all that high-quality plastic?"

Rainart paused to finish chewing a tender morsel of beetle. "I have a new mine," he stated calmly.

"Well, congratulations. Where is it?"

Rainart paused again to eat another bee's wing and drink half a mug of ale. "About thirty-five d-units north and a bit east of the old one."

"Thirty-five d-units north? Isn't there one of those ignorant ant colonies there?" Ragnar refilled their mugs.

Rainart chewed, swallowed, and drained the mug again. No need to keep it a secret any more. "Yes, there is an ant colony there. Now it's my colony and my mine. Hard workers, too—hence the increase in production."

Ragnar's mandibles opened wide. "When old Sir Richard tried that, he lost every single one of his warriors!"

Rainart chewed, happy with having the upper pod at the moment. "That's because old Richard was foolish and attacked a fire ant colony. Mine are very placid dairying ants—practically no defenses, and smart enough not to get themselves killed. Oh, and there is no meat as tender as those grasshoppers they raise. I really must have you to dinner at my home soon to enjoy some with me." He was truly enjoying the look of renewed respect in his adversary's eyes.

"I would like that immensely—and the conversation with your lovely mate."

Rainart didn't believe that any more than he had the first "compliment." Ragnar probably wanted to pump for more information about how Rainart had gotten his ant colony, which he wasn't about to divulge.

The two finished their meal and the keg of ale. Rainart sensed that Ragnar was about to ask more questions, so he called to Rand. "See if you can find that server and tell him we're ready for some entertainment now." He turned to Ragnar, "My treat; I insist."

Twelfth Time Frame, 19 B.C.C.

Daeira and Delana stood at the colony's main entrance and watched the roach families leave. Females followed their males, carrying bundles and often a tiny caged nymph. Older nymphs followed their mothers. They did not look happy.

Rashad smiled and told Daeira and Delana, "Sir Rainart says there is work for them now in Roacheria. I told you in the beginning that having the workers and their families was temporary."

"Then why aren't you and the warriors leaving, too?" Delana asked.

"I never said that Sir Rainart's ownership of this colony and the plastic mine were temporary. You continue to belong to him. The warriors will stay, and probably more will come, to make sure you do what you are told. Sir Rainart will now collect 60 percent of what you mine instead of half."

"But…you said that plastic was the workers' pay and for their young!" Daeira shouted.

"That was true; they did get a small portion of plastic for their pay to provide for their young. The rest of the plastic has always gone to Sir Rainart."

A moment of silence followed while Delana and Daeira realized what his statements meant. An uncomfortable feeling of anger rose in Daeira. She wanted to bite him in some vulnerable area—even though he was larger than she was. But it would do no good. She dared not speak for fear she would lose control.

Delana, her role as Council Chief overcoming her personal feelings managed to say, "Forty percent of what we mine is not enough for all our families! You assured us that if we submitted to Sir Rainart, we would live and have plastic for every colony member, not just our young."

Rashad rose to his full height, which he had room to do in the larger entrance tunnel, towering over both of them. "You flashed the green pennant. You agreed to our control. Sir Rainart will take

60 percent of what you mine! If the other 40 percent is not enough, tell your workers to produce more so that the total is more, and your percentage gives you enough!"

He walked away before the two female ants could say another word.

18 B.C.C. (15 O.R.)

Sir Rainart personally opened the portal of his elaborate estate to Sir Ragnar and his mate. Six time frames had passed since their previous meeting. "Come in, come in. Sorry it has taken me so long to follow up on that tasty meal of roast grasshopper I promised you."

The two female roaches greeted each other cordially. Rainart's mate tugged at her friend's front pod, "Let me show you the new piece of art Rainart bought me!" The two ambled away to a second parlor on the mansion's main floor, leaving the two males to their business before the meal.

Sir Rainart poured a mug of ale for his guest.

"Here's to investing in ant colonies," Sir Ragnar said, raising his mug in salute. "I thought about what you said the last time we met and went and got one for myself—little colony about fifteen d-units north of my current mine—which is still producing, by the way. Only I didn't take over a season cycle to do it, wasting time and resources on an interpreter like you did—yes, I've heard how you accomplished your deal. The dairying colony I've got now wasn't nearly as populous as yours, but there's a fairly good mine there. My invasion was quick and decisive—simply slaughtered them all. I had no problem finding enough workers either. They didn't even have to build their flimsy shacks—just moved into the upper levels of the ant chambers underground. They aren't complaining, either. Some of my newest hires used to work for you, I think. They sure knew what to do in ant tunnels! My thanks to you."

Ragnar's criticism of Rainart's method of gaining control stung him to the core, but he managed a cordial grin. They clinked their mugs together and drained them.

"Perhaps," Rainart said after draining a second mug, "we should keep our ant colony take-overs between the two of us for now. We wouldn't want too much competition in that arena, would we?"

"Good point, good point indeed," Ragnar said. "Yes, just between us. You and I have been rivals for too long. It's time for an alliance."

A servant entered at that moment to announce that dinner was ready. Later in the evening, Rainart agreed to an alliance, but he remained wary of his former adversary.

9.

Eighth Time Frame, 295 C.C.I., Henry Roach-Dairier II

Reading in Rainart's Journal about that evening visit between the two roaches, alarmed me greatly. No one had ever known about a colony completely destroyed by roaches— all of its members slaughtered in mass murder. It wasn't that I didn't believe it, but I felt I had to have some other factual evidence or others, ant or roach, might not believe me. The report of the conversation between Sir Rainart and Sir Ragnar that evening was the only mention of this ant colony in Rainart's journal. After sharing the passage with the archivist at Fire 2 (and knowing more revisions in my outline might follow), I returned to Roacheria to search for any records concerning Sir Ragnar I might have missed.

The archives would not be the place to begin my search since official roach records barely acknowledged that period of Roachstory. I headed instead for the library to search old maps for indications of where Sir Ragnar's legitimate mine had been and what might have been fifteen d-units north.

I also went to visit Rabiah and Raissa since their home was on the way to the library. "Welcome back, Henry. It's so good to see you, but sooner than I expected," Rabiah said.

"Sooner than I expected, too." I showed her the passage in the precious journal she had found and loaned to me and told her what I was searching for now.

Raissa joined us, and I had to explain things to her, too.

She read the passage again and then said, "I read through this rather quickly before. Now that I read it again, it is very upsetting indeed! You know, Mother, we stopped searching once we found the journal. We should sort through all those old documents again carefully. We might find something more. How dreadful to think such a thing actually happened!"

"Are you staying at your home again?" Rabiah asked. "I will send you a message the moment we find any other letters or documents."

"Yes, I am at home in Meadow Commonwealth," I replied. "I don't mean to hurry off right now, but the library closes at four in the afternoon on Seconddays. I probably won't find any maps or documents right away, but I need to introduce myself there. I should let them know what I'm searching for and that they can expect to see me frequently."

"Please come again soon," Raissa said taking both my pods in hers. "I've really missed our visits."

"I have missed our visits, too. I promise I'll come again as soon as I can."

I hurried on to the library. It was already three in the afternoon, but I would at least have a chance to present my credentials and meet with the head librarian. The receptionist was rather cool toward me, but ushered me to the head librarian's office. I placed my credentials before him along with a letter from my mother since she was a board member. He reached forward so slowly I thought he might never pick up the parchments. I couldn't describe him as elderly; ancient seemed a better word.

The head librarian looked me over carefully and studied the papers. His expression softened. "Your grandfather used to spend a lot of time in here. I was still in training, but I often came with my father, who was head librarian before me. I was fascinated by your grandfather, especially since my father seemed to stiffen up every time he saw your grandfather back when he was a young counselor of law. Back then, I had to hide my true feelings about ant/roach relations; I know you understand. What is it you are looking for?"

I spent several minutes—all the time there was—explaining my research. He nodded. "It's almost closing time, but arrive as soon as we open tomorrow. We will search together."

Twelfth Time Frame, 18 B.C.C.

The members of South Dairy 1 had mixed feelings about the roach families' departure. In wordless ways, those who worked in the plastic mine had developed caring feelings for the roach workers. They had noticed that the roaches were always tense whenever Rashad was around. The ants had seen him punish the roaches on more than one occasion. They particularly disliked the way Rashad stamped down his strong back pods on the back of a worker lying prone before him. To ants, such a practice seemed very cruel. They could barely find a word to describe it. Those who worked closely with the roaches had come to understand that life was very difficult for such workers in Roacheria. They had sensed how thankful these families were to be working in the ant colony. They began to understand the ever-present sadness in the roach families' faces. Others were glad to have the roach families gone, thinking it might lead to the warriors leaving, too.

Everyone was dismayed over the announcement that the colony's supply of plastic would be reduced. The Colony Council asked that two workers from each area be sent to the plastic mine to replace the roaches who were no longer there. Each work area was also asked to send a third volunteer to help increase production enough to cover the colony's needs. Every area would need to work a little harder to help those in the mines to get back the additional 10 percent the roaches would now be taking.

"An extra h-unit per day from everyone will provide what we need while spreading the work load equally," Council Chief Delana's communication read. That didn't seem so bad.

Another hundred roach warriors who didn't seem to do anything besides stand around and demand their share of food arrived to live in the roach quarters. They loomed over everyone in every area of the colony. But the ants adjusted and life went on. Master Daeira and Council Chief Delana and all the council members rotated around the colony, spending one day each quarter time frame working alongside colony members, setting an example by their own increased labors, and encouraging everyone else.

Rashad knew that Sir Rainart would make another visit to the colony at the beginning of the next season cycle. He explained to Daeira and Delana that he would be punished (and it was true) if the two of them didn't show proper respect to Sir Rainart. The two females agreed to a small show of respect.

"Sir Rainart," Rashad said, stooping very low and remaining prone until his employer told him to rise, "please, may I have a word with you in private before we tour the operations?"

Sir Rainart grunted and agreed. The two went into Rashad's domicile.

"Sir, I'm thinking you plan to up the percentage of plastic again this year?"

"Of course. Why?"

"Well, and you know my ideas have paid off for you before, so I'd like to suggest a way you might have even more profit. After all, if the market gets glutted with too much plastic, the price drops, correct?"

Another grunt from Sir Rainart.

Rashad took a deep breath. "I've noticed that many of the guards don't have enough to do and they are always complaining about a lack of females. In addition, the ants are accepting everything and cause very little trouble. We haven't had to use the mantis compound for about four time frames—and when we have, it has been roach warrior, never an ant. Some warriors have actually taken to hunting wild beetles to feed them. So you could send at least 100 warriors back to Roacheria—a lot less cost right there. The others could be rotated more frequently so they don't become bored and cause the commander trouble."

He paused, noticing that Sir Rainart was rubbing his mandibles with one front pod—a good sign.

"Then, all of the warriors get their food free here, and a place to live, which they would have to pay for if they were in Roacheria. You could start charging them for room and board out of their pay—more credit in your accounts!"

Sir Rainart began pacing about Rashad's parlor. Rashad knew that meant he was thinking seriously about this proposal.

Rashad dared to speak further. "If I have this good news to tell the ants, I'm sure you'll see an increase in productivity. You don't have to decide right now. Let me take you around the colony to see how well things are going."

They went to meet with the council first. As agreed, Delana and Daeira nodded their heads, antennae lowered—but not their bodies—until Sir Rainart tipped his antennae.

Rashad spoke up quickly. "Master Daeira, Council Chief Delana, thank you for your time today. I have good news for you! Sir Rainart will leave the percentage of plastic the same as it has been! Plus, some of the warriors will be leaving. Isn't that wonderful? Perhaps you could express your gratitude with another show of respect?"

It was quite a risk announcing this before Sir Rainart had made the decision, but the look on the two female ants' faces—true gratitude—was sure to help influence his decision. Rashad's gamble paid off. The two smiled, said thank you, and stooped, brushing their front pods briefly to the sides.

"They say thank you for your visit," Rashad said to Rainart.

Sir Rainart tipped his antennae and they rose.

"Shall we proceed on our tour?" Rashad coaxed.

Delana and Daeira followed the two roaches quietly throughout the colony looking at each other from time to time with questioning looks that each understood to mean they would talk in private once the tour was over.

Sir Rainart was properly impressed with the state of his colony. As they headed back toward the main entrance, Sir Rainart stated, "Much better than last year. The percentage of plastic will remain the same." He stopped short of any more compliments to his interpreter's ideas but finished with, "I'll need to spend some time with the warrior commander before I leave."

Half an h-unit later, Sir Rainart left the colony with his personal warrior escort. Rashad jotted in his journal: Why do I keep jeopardizing my own welfare for these puny ants? I don't understand what comes over me sometimes. But at least it turned out all right.

Things continued to go well in the ant colony, so Sir Rainart didn't return for several season cycles. His accounts were bursting. The overall price of plastic rose after he and other mine owners had a formal meeting in which they reached agreement to reduce production by 5 percent. The ants were more content with fewer warriors and had become accustomed to working one h-unit longer each day. By the twelfth season cycle of roach occupation, many ants had forgotten what life was like when their colony was their own.

10.

Eighth Time Frame, 295 C.C.I., Henry Roach-Dairier II

I was at the portal to Roacheria's main library when it opened the next morning. The head librarian welcomed me. As he led me to the map room, his movements were so awkward that I asked him if he needed assistance.

"No thank you," he replied. "The day I stop moving will be the day I die."

We went on to a room on the top level where ancient and newer maps were stored. He pulled out three: the most recent, the oldest the facility had, and another drawn shortly after the time when South and East Roacheria came together.

"I arrived earlier and began the search," he told me. "I think these will be what we need." He unrolled the maps onto a large table in the room and weighed down the corners with small woven sacks filled with sand.

We looked at the oldest first, locating Sir Ragnar's mine. I found the scale and measured the number of d-units mentioned in the journal. Holding a measuring tool with one end on that mine, we carefully marked off a fifteen d-unit circle around it. We could not, of course, write on the map, so we laid out string. I took parchment and ink and listed all the landmarks within the circle and their distances from the mine.

We repeated this process on the second map. Some of the landmarks were no longer within the circle. I rubbed one front pod over my outer mandible and said, "There's a lot of discrepancy here."

"That's to be expected. Measurements were not so accurate way back then; plus, maps were not always drawn exactly to scale. But we should be able to note enough landmarks to see basically where things are and find them on the newer map."

Thus, we proceeded to a recent map—which would also be the most accurate. Two of the landmarks remained. I had brought a new map of my own that I would be able to write on. Ragnar's original mine in Roacheria still showed up on it. That mine had remained in his clan's possession and continued to produce as recently as fifty season cycles ago before it finally played out. The other landmarks, two prominent duo pod ruins, seemed to have "shifted" from the old to the new map but would be easy to find when someone could actually go to the sites. From these, we would try to get an expert to run straight surveying lines, and where the lines crossed, perhaps find some physical evidence of the lost colony.

"Now I need to find a reputable surveyor," I said.

"Be careful out there. That area is still controlled by the same clan. They might not like the idea of you poking around on their surface."

"I will be careful, and thank you so very much for your help."

That had not taken nearly as long as had I thought it might. I would have ample time to visit my mother's office in the SERCB building to see what permissions might be needed.

Mother was quiet for a few minutes once I showed her the markings on my map and described what I hoped to do.

"You may have to be patient for a while. Permits for archeological digs—which is what this would be—take time. I know a good surveyor who will help you because he owes me a favor. You didn't get anywhere with Ragnar's descendants, did you?"

"No, my letters were returned and a servant slammed the portal in my face."

"I thought as much. They will do everything in their power, which is considerable, to prevent a search if they know you are the one behind it."

I sighed.

"But, I have friends in archeology, too," Mother added. "They might approach the family with the idea that the ruin still standing might indicate more beneath the surface that might have value. Any artifacts found belong to the surface owner. That might tempt them. I don't know how long all this will take, so you might as well head back to Fire 2."

I gave my mother an affectionate embrace. "Thanks."

I spent the rest of that day with Raissa and her mother and left for Fire 2 the following morning.

Twelfth Time Frame, 18 B.C.C.

A few days after the changes in the ant's work hours, two young adults, Dodie and Dart, stood before family and friends for their mating ceremony.

Dodie and Dart's parents carried them in separate baskets to the main meditation chamber. They spoke words very similar to those currently in use. Dart, as the male, said his promise first. "I come to you now to begin to fulfill our promise. I will cherish and support you no matter what joys or sorrows may occur. I will nurture both physically and emotionally all new life that may come from our union. I promise this freely as long as we both live in this world."

Dodie repeated the same words to Dart. No giving of symbolic gifts occurred back then. The two rose, joined middle pods, raised their front pods above their heads, and said to the other ants gathered to celebrate with them: "To each other we have given ourselves. To you, fellow colony members, we give our talents and our work. Confirm our gifts and pledge to us your help in anything we cannot do for ourselves."

Colony members responded, "We accept your gifts and pledge our support to both of you."

They entered their names in the colony's Record of the Mated. Everyone moved into the adjoining banquet room where a whole roasted grasshopper lay waiting to be carved and served to those present. The two passed out mugs of fermented honeydew. When everyone had eaten their fill, musicians entered with reed flutes and peapod shakers. The dancing began.

After the dancing ended, the two climbed into one basket to be carried by both sets of parents to their new home. However, because everyone had to work longer hours under the new schedule, their Mating Holiday was limited to three days instead of the usual quarter time frame.

Two time frames later, Dodie laid her first egg. When her son hatched, she named him Duncan after her grandfather.

Fifth Time Frame, 17 B.C.C.

Master Daeira had another very troubling vision. In the vivid dream, she saw many parents wailing in grief over young adults emerging from pupation with exoskeletons that fractured at the slightest bump and with no intelligence—classic symptoms of severe plastic deprivation! The young adults died within a few days. Plastic deprivation rarely happened in an ant colony because giving their young enough plastic was such a high priority. About the only time it occurred was when the mechanical devices set up to nourish young during pupation failed. Sometimes such a failure happened late in pupation and the loss of intelligence was only slight. Such young adults could still be trained for simpler jobs around the colony. The real tragedy was that these plastic-deprived young rarely lived over five season cycles into adulthood.

Daeira left her domicile quietly as soon as she awoke, looked both ways down the tunnel, twitched her antennae to see whether anyone was about, and used smaller, less-traveled tunnels to reach Council Chief Delana's domicile. For the last season cycle, Rashad seemed to know whenever she and Delana met and insisted on being present. He attended every council meeting, too.

Daeira did not even tap at the portal, but let herself into Delana's domicile as silently as possible. Delana was still asleep on her cushion. Daeira placed her front pods on the sides of Delana's mandibles, holding them so she could not make a sound. Then she tapped Delana's thorax with a middle pod.

Delana, jumped at the touch, awoke wide-eyed. Daeira hushed her and then whispered. "I'm sorry to startle you, but I must tell you something, and I could not take the chance that Rashad would be with us."

"What is wrong?" Delana whispered back.

"I've had a terrible vision. I think it is a warning from Essence." She told the council chief about her dream and then they discussed what to do about it.

"Do you think the roaches would actually stop allowing us all plastic?" Delana asked, raising her front pods in dismay.

"I don't know, but they've reduced our percentage and do not let any plastic accumulate in storage against emergency. The dream is a warning—a strong one. Somehow we must prepare, and Rashad cannot know about it. I have no more trust in him."

Delana paced about her tiny parlor. She no longer whispered, but her voice was low. "It's been shown before that once we reach adulthood, we no longer need plastic. Only the young really need it. All adults must continue to draw their shares, but they cannot consume it. Everyone must hide every bit of plastic possible. Perhaps it will never be needed, but…."

"I agree," Daeira said. "We must dig little spaces between our walls and under our floors to store it. The diggings must be smoothed out, and the storage places covered so Rashad, or any of the warriors who sometimes enter our homes unannounced, will not be able to see any telltale sign."

Delana stopped pacing and took Daeira's pods in hers. "But how will we be able to tell this to everyone without Rashad learning of it? We can't use the emergency communications network. He knows how that works."

"Essence did not reveal that to me."

"You had better get back to your home. It will be rising time for everyone in a few moments. I'll get word to you somehow."

Daeira crept along a different route than she had come, one that took her by the smallest tunnels until she reached a spot near the colony's entrance. She turned down the main tunnel and met Rashad on his way up.

"Good morning, Rashad."

"You're about early!"

"I woke in the night and could not go back to sleep. So I went to the surface to meditate."

"Oh. How's the weather out there?"

Daeira's vague answer was, "The usual for this time of the season cycle."

He went on his way, saying no more.

Three days later, Daeira's assistant returned from an errand. "This is a memorized message from Council Chief Delana:

From this time onward, adults are not to eat plastic. Master Daeira has had a vision that warns us that the roaches might deny us all plastic. We must prepare. Continue to collect your allotment as if nothing is different. Dig a storage compartment under your floor, or behind a wall. Spread out the earth from the digging, and cover the storage compartment, so no one who enters will see it. If the vision is fulfilled, we may be able to feed our young.

Once she had delivered the memorized message, Daeira's assistant told her how the new communication system would work. "Council Chief Delana consulted with the colony job manager. Together, they worked out a new network based on those with whom we work and those we live near. That way, neither Rashad nor any roach warrior will be suspicious of a conversation. It will be two coworkers talking or two neighbors exchanging greetings or spending time in each other's company. Anytime we need to get out an urgent request or message, this is how we will do it."

Daeira smiled at her assistant. The ant who had given the message to her assistant was one of those she shared meals with regularly. Daeira was to pass the message to the two families on the right of her domicile and the three on her left. She saw them every day and often shared meals with them.

"Did Delana mention anything about how I should communicate with her?"

"Yes, she said you are to tell me, and I will tell my father, who will tell her next door neighbor, who will pass it on to her. She also said that from now on, you should only see her at council meetings."

Daeira and her assistant then proceeded with their usual tasks. Before the h-unit was up, Rashad arrived for his customary Thirdday visit. He had nothing new to tell her, and she resented the intrusion on her time.

Dodie's father brought the message to her and Dart that evening. They were to pass it to the rest of those who cared for the grasshopper herds. They had their secret plastic compartment completed before they went to bed. They passed the instructions quietly to their coworkers as they moved among the grasshopper herd.

11.

Sixth Time Frame, 17 B.C.C.

Sir Rainart sat in his board office pondering what lay ahead for him. He wasn't getting any younger, and his physician had given him some unwelcome news the previous day. He had no son to train to take over his business. His only daughter had mated and given him two male grandnymphs, but Rainart was not particularly fond of his son-in-law. Granted, he was a top-notch professional who did consulting work for the city's major builders. He had been a good mate for Rainart's daughter, but he was related to Ragnar. When a female mated, she became part of her mate's family and clan. Rainart and Ragnar had maintained their alliance for many season cycles, but when Rainart thought about it, his son-in-law had begun courting his daughter not long after the alliance began.

He had always hoped his mate would lay another egg, but she was way beyond the fertile time of her life. To whom would he pass on his legacy? How would he keep it out of Ragnar's pods?

As he was thinking about this, his assistant tapped on the portal.

"What is it?" Rainart asked.

"Sir, fellow Board Member Sir Ragnar would like a few moments of your time."

Why does he always show up at moments like this? Rainart thought. He sighed. "Send him in."

Ragnar greeted Rainart pleasantly, inquiring after his mate and daughter. Rainart was polite in return, and then brushed aside formalities with, "I've got a lot to do. What's on your mind, Ragnar?"

"Always have appreciated your directness, my old friend."

Friend, my abdominal hole, Rainart thought.

Ragnar continued. "I have three sons and two mines. I would like to buy you out and turn your operations over to my youngest son when he comes of age. I'm sure you would like to retire soon and have fewer responsibilities. I know I plan to retire once my sons are thoroughly trained and ready to take over. In fact, my oldest is already managing my newer mine. What do you think? After all, whom have you got to turn it over to?"

Rainart didn't reply immediately, calling instead to his assistant to bring some refreshments—an expected courtesy.

"What makes you think I'm ready to retire?" he asked, once the tankard of ale had been poured into mugs.

"I hate to be blunt, but I've noticed at the last few board meetings that you move as if your joints are bothering you. You've got a good decade of season cycles on me, and after all, none of us will live forever."

Rainart took another glug of ale. Stiff, painful leg joints were the least of his medical problems. "I thought you didn't like to be blunt."

"No offense intended. It's just that you could ensure the futures of all your clan's offspring with the price I have in mind." He placed a piece of parchment before Rainart with a price so high that Rainart nearly choked on his ale.

"I'm inclined to say no, but I will think about it," Rainart said after catching his breath.

"Of course. Take your time. I can wait...."

Rainart knew the unspoken words: Until you're dead and then I'll have my law counselor remind your family that your daughter and grandnymphs are part of my clan under the law.

Ragnar had Rainart in a vice, and both of them knew it.

Ragnar graciously ended the meeting. "Still joining us for dinner at our home next Seventhday?"

"Yes, of course. My mate mentioned that she's looking forward to it."

"Until then." Ragnar rose, bowed, and left.

Rainart left all the work he had to do behind and headed for his law counselor's office, which was not far away. Even if he accepted Ragnar's offer, Ragnar would get it all back when Rainart died. He had to find a way to keep that fortune out of the pods of Ragnar's clan.

Rainart left his counselor's office much happier. The following

Seventhday, he signed the agreement with Ragnar. Less than a time frame later, his daughter's new egg hatched—a female.

Five time frames after that, Rainart died when his breathing organs gave out.

Ninth Time Frame, 295 C.C.I.

I had been back in Fire 2 only a quarter time frame when, to my complete surprise, my mother arrived to see me. After a quick embrace, she laid three parchments before me.

"Rabiah and Raissa came to see me yesterday and brought me these. I knew you would want them right away."

The first parchment was Sir Rainart's copy of the agreement to sell his ant colony and its plastic mine to Sir Ragnar. Across it, Sir Rainart had scrawled in large letters: ABDOMINAL HOLE, I'LL GET YOU IN THE END, which must have been added after the agreement was signed by both parties.

The second document was a copy of Sir Rainart's last wishes. It stated that all of his assets—and most importantly the funds from his agreement with Sir Ragnar—would be placed in a trust to be distributed only to females of all future generations at a set amount per time frame in perpetuity. So the two grandsons Rainart had from his daughter would receive nothing since they belonged to Ragnar's clan through the mating. The granddaughter recently hatched at that time would get everything. It named Rainart's trusted legal counselor and his descendants as managers of the trust.

The third document was a decree of the "legal ending" of Rainart's daughter's mating.

I stared at the three documents and then at my mother.

"Rabiah said to tell you that they checked into all the hatching and mating records since that time. Rainart died of degenerating breathing organs. Apparently, he had been sick for quite a while. It seems that Rainart's daughter's mate legally abandoned her when the provisions of Rainart's will became known. He took the two sons since they were legally part of his clan, but he was angry because he would receive none of the money Ragnar had paid for that mine. Rainart's daughter moved back into the house she had grown up in and took care of her mother and daughter."

I shook my antennae in astonishment.

Mother went on. "Not only that, but when that daughter grew up and mated, her mate abandoned her when he found out that under the provisions of the trust, he would never personally own any of the wealth."

"From daughter to daughter to daughter, right down to Rabiah," I said.

"Rabiah's mate was one of a few in all the generations who chose to live in Rainart's family domicile. There were only three males who did not abandon their mates because of the trust. Rabiah's mate was one of the three. He also died of breathing organ degeneration—younger than most to be struck with that ailment."

We sat in silence for several minutes.

Finally, Mother spoke again. "Raissa asked me to bring you this personal letter. You can read it later. I hate to come so far and leave immediately, but I've got a client going before the Chief Enforcer in the morning."

"I'm amazed you came yourself instead of sending these by messenger." For even the fastest roach, it was a five-h-unit trip.

"From the little you've shared with me, I knew these documents would be keys to understanding the entire unfortunate time. I didn't trust anyone else to deliver them. Don't worry. I'll get back in time. My young assistant carried me to you and colony members here have a couple of baskets waiting to return us to Meadow Commonwealth."

I gave her another embrace and she headed back home. Then I tore open the letter from Raissa:

My cherished Henry,

When Mother and I found and read the documents your mother has just given you, I knew you must have them immediately. I wanted to come myself, but Mother said it would not be proper for a single female roach to enter an ant colony unaccompanied. She is soooo old-fashioned in many ways, but I cherish her for that.

The documents explained so much that we had always wondered about. In some ways, I feel an almost overwhelming guilt to think that some twelve generations of mothers and daughters have lived comfortably off the work of those early ants while they and their young suffered so much. On the other pod, those same mothers and daughters would have had no protection under Roacherian law. I also find it ironic that no sons after that first generation ever hatched to any of Rainart's descendants.

It also made us realize why I was attacked as a nymph. I've never told you about that, but I am now. I was almost twelve, about to make my final molt. Mother had taken me to our physician for more pain relievers. On the way home, a huge male—warrior-trained—attacked us. He knocked my mother unconscious but left her otherwise uninjured. Then he gouged my face. He was about to crush me when enforcers heard my screams and came to our assistance. The attacker ran off and never was caught.

Now, I believe the attack on me was an attempt to prevent the beginning of another generation of our family. I can guess who was behind it.

I hope to see you again soon.

Yours,
Raissa

I put my head down and wept.

Fourth Time Frame, 16 B.C.C.

Rashad had written in his journal: I got official word in Eleventh Time Frame last season cycle that Sir Rainart died, and Sir Ragnar now owns this mine. I wonder how long it will be before he comes to visit. Will I still have a job?

Sir Ragnar waited several time frames, for it was the custom to allow a family time to grieve in private before the distribution of assets after a death.

It was with much pomp and ceremony that Sir Ragnar arrived shortly after Summer Solstice. Rashad stooped very low and spread out his pods. "Welcome, Sir. I am Rashad, the interpreter. May I take you to my domicile to explain my role and how things have been done here all these season cycles?"

"No. I prefer to see the entire operation first. Then I will tell you how things will be run."

His tone of voice made it plain that Rashad should not argue. "Very good, Sir. Please follow me."

Rashad led his new master first to the roach area of the colony. He pointed out the many domiciles and the two dorms for warriors.

"Why are so many unoccupied?" Sir Ragnar asked.

Rashad kept his head down and answered, "When there were more warriors, they got into trouble with each other. The ants were doing as they should and more were not needed. Those here got along better when it was not so crowded, so Sir Rainart left it that way."

"Humph!"

They then proceeded through various tunnels down to the mine. Sir Ragnar nodded but said nothing.

From there, Rashad took him to the colony market area and explained how carefully the ant rations of plastic were given out and recorded. "I've always done this myself on Fifthdays," he said with some pride. "My records are in perfect order."

Sir Ragnar looked around at the other market stalls where ants chose various foods and a few other products—crockery jugs for honeydew, small cloths for washing, pots, plates and mugs, etc.—used in their homes. "This is the entire market?"

"Yes, Sir. Ants live simply. They don't need anything else."

Ragnar twanged his mandible in disgust.

"Let me show you the surface area where they graze their grasshoppers and take care of aphids."

Ragnar seemed to be impressed with the surface industries. Rashad suggested they return to his domicile for lunch, where he presented his new master with slices of cold roast grasshopper and his largest mug filled with honeydew. "I'm sorry there is not time to up warm the meat," he said pointing to a cooking box.

Ragnar chewed the grasshopper slowly. "Hummm, such very tender meat. I remember it from a couple of dinners with Sir Rainart before he died. I must be sure to have some delivered to my home on a regular basis."

The portal opened unexpectedly. A surprised ant set down a large container of water and picked up any empty one. "I'm sorry, Rashad. You aren't usually at home at delivery time."

"It's all right. Thank you," Rashad said in Ant. The water delivery ant turned and left.

"What was that all about?" Ragnar asked.

"Every day, that ant delivers my supply of water. That's his job, and that of several others, to take water to each family every day. I ladle out some for drinking and use the rest to bathe in the evening. Someone else comes after I leave in the morning and picks up the used bath water. They reuse it in the pottery-making chamber and other areas of the colony where pure drinking water is not necessary."

Ragnar shook his head. Rashad couldn't tell whether it was in amazement or disgust.

"I want to see those production areas, too."

Rashad spent a good bit of the afternoon showing Sir Ragnar the special areas of the colony where the ants manufactured the simple things they required for their lives and the water system.

When that ended, Sir Ragnar said, "Now assemble them so I can tell them what I want."

"Yes, Sir. Of course, you will not see the entire colony. They have a group called the Colony Council, and a second group of about 100 who then pass information on to everyone else."

"Fine. Send word for fifty warriors to be there, too."

"Warriors? What for?"

"Don't ask questions. Just do it!"

Rashad brought Sir Ragnar to the Council Chamber and told him to make himself comfortable on one of the benches. "It will take about a quarter h-unit to assemble all of them." He left to find Delana, whom he had not informed earlier about the death of Sir Rainart. Things could become awkward, to say the least.

Once in Delana's work chamber, he said, "You've probably heard that I've been directing an important SRCB Board Member around the colony," he said.

"Yes, but why hasn't Sir Rainart come?"

There was no good way to say it, so Rashad lied. "It has come as a complete shock to me, but Sir Ragnar—whom you are about to meet—has told me that Sir Rainart passed away. Sir Ragnar now owns this colony. He requests an assembly to tell you how he will run things. Please gather the Council at once and the messengers. Delana, please, show some respect. I will return to the Council Chamber and wait for you there."

"I must inform Master Daeira, too."

"Just hurry. Sir Ragnar is not one to displease or disrespect."

Master Daeira was meditating when Delana arrived. There were tears in the Spiritual Guide's eyes.

"Master Daeira, you must come to the Council Chamber. It seems we have a new roach claiming ownership of our colony. Rashad requests our presence."

Daeira's pods shook. "I know. Essence...." She broke down weeping.

"Is it what you feared?"

Daeira nodded.

Delana quickly fixed her a cup of herb tea, which Daeira glugged down so she could regain control before they went to the Council Chambers.

By the time Council Chief Delana and Master Daeira reached the Council Chamber, the fifty warriors stood in a ring around the chamber's circular wall. The other council members and message bearers sat in the center on the rows of benches. The two females took their places in front of the assembled ants. Phenomes of anxiety floated about to be absorbed by everyone's antennae.

Rashad brought Sir Ragnar to stand in front of the two females. He did not introduce them, but hissed to the two females, "Please, lower yourselves!"

The glares from the roach warriors were so frightening that Delana and Daeira did as they were told.

Sir Ragnar turned to Rashad and said in Roach. "Tell them exactly what I say."

"Yes, Sir," Rashad said, also stooping low.

"You may rise."

Rashad translated as Sir Ragnar spoke. "Sir Rainart sold this mine to me several time frames before he died. I have been generous in waiting this long to come. As he owned all of you, so, now, do I. You will continue to work as you have but now all plastic belongs to me and if any ant tries to take any, that ant will be killed. More warriors will arrive, and in fact are waiting for my signal, to see that my wishes are carried out."

Rashad, with shaking antennae and voice, delivered the message in Ant.

The ants' mandibles opened in shock. Six council members rose and shouted, "We must have plastic for our young! Sir Rainart assured us—" but before they could finish, warriors grabbed the six who shouted and bit off their heads.

Shrieks rose from the rest of the assembled ants.

Master Daeira lifted shaking front pods and cried out to Essence, "The day of the green pennant was the worst of my life until now! Essence, help us!"

Delana threw herself at the pods of Sir Ragnar and Rashad, totally prone, begging for mercy for the colony's young.

Rashad, as stunned as any of the ants, but seeing the look in Sir Ragnar's eyes, dared not speak on their behalf.

Sir Ragnar placed his back pod on Delana's thorax but pressed down only hard enough to establish his complete authority over her and thereby the entire colony. "I am not Sir Rainart. Never forget that!"

Rashad's voice shook again as he translated the statement.

Sir Ragnar's next words were for Rashad. "You'll keep your job and your present rate of pay as long as you keep them compliant. My new warriors will move into those empty quarters. They'll see that the mantis compound is regularly used—the mantises can eat you, too, if need be. I don't need you. I don't need any of them. That female's act of respect is the only reason any of you are still alive."

Then he signaled his personal warriors and marched out of the colony.

12.

Fourth Time Frame, 16 B.C.C.

The shock of the murders hung in the air for several moments after Sir Ragnar left the Council Chamber. The contingent of warriors remained in place. Neither Master Daeira nor Council Chief Delana knew whether they should even move.

Finally, Rashad spoke. "Please, rise. Go ahead and remove your dead. Only their immediate families should attend the covering. I...I did not expect this." Then he spoke to the warriors in Roach. "Let the ants cover their dead. Watch only from a distance, please."

The warrior commander gave a curt nod with his antennae.

The ants moved as if in a daze. No one spoke while in Rashad's presence that day. In silence, council members carefully picked up their murdered members' heads and bodies. Others went for water and cleaning tools to remove the pools of life juice. Stains remained on the hardened earthen floor of the Council Chamber for many season cycles. The roaches insisted the stains stay there to keep fear in the hearts of the ants, but to the ants, the stains honored the fallen.

Messenger ants did what they always did: inform the colony of the horrible events of that day. Roach warriors seemed to be everywhere as the news was passed from one group in the colony to another. It was always received with shocked expressions on the faces of the ants, followed by silence.

The "secret" communication system, however, was buzzing with strong emotions. Many colony members felt they should band together and fight back, for although the roach warriors were larger, swifter, and had huge mandibles, adult colony members (male and female) still outnumbered them by something around fifty to one.

In their domicile, Dodie and Dart, parents of Duncan, clung to each other weeping. Dodie had been part of the messenger group for about two season cycles. She had repeated all day what had happened, but in her own home, she found she could not speak. When she finally could, she said, "We have enough plastic hidden for Duncan to last through his pupation—if it has to. We have enough from the last market day for today. We will begin to use our hidden supplies of plastic tomorrow."

Dart embraced her and stroked her antennae. Not long after Dodie changed jobs from herding the grasshoppers to delivering messages, there had been a small collapse in the mine tunnel where she had delivered the news of the day. Ant doctors had saved her life and patched up her crushed abdomen, but they were not able to save her future eggs. The pair had mourned the fact that there would be no other young besides Duncan.

"I never thought," Dart began, "that I would consider your accident a blessing. But there would not have been enough plastic for another young one. Forgive me if saying so brings back the pain of loss."

Dodie shook her head sadly. "There will always be pain at the thought, but I know you are right. There must be a way to rid ourselves of these roaches, but not the way some of our members are talking about. Let us raise our thoughts to Essence to reveal it to us."

Many such conversations took place throughout the colony. Without need for any announcement from the council, ants began to feed the hidden supplies of plastic to their young.

Some families thought they had enough plastic hidden. Others knew they didn't. Families past egg-laying age pledged to pass their hidden supplies to those in need. Each family dug a tiny hole between their domicile and those on either side so that plastic could be given from one to another without it being seen by roach warriors, who now watched their every move in any tunnel. An assessment of hidden supplies reached Council Chief Delana showing a sufficient amount remained for all current young. But if more eggs were laid....

With a heavy heart, Delana sent out instructions through the secret network:

Until such time as we can rid ourselves of our oppressors, I must ask that young adults who are single remain so. If you have made a promise, please, do not unite until we can be sure of plastic supplies. Remain in a state of promise. If you have not made a promise with someone, do not make a promise to mate. Those who are mated, do not feel guilty if you lay another egg. You made your promise in faith that plastic would be there for you to nourish your young. The present circumstances are beyond your control. But it would be a great moral wrong for any adults to mate now, knowing they cannot supply their young with plastic. I know this is a great sacrifice, but it must be made.

Tenth Time Frame, 16 B.C.C.

The secret communication system put out the word that they would attack the roaches and drive them from the colony. But one worker (only a fourth of the way along the system) was waylaid at his job and failed to pass on the message. So the vast majority of colony adults did not know when and where the attack on the roaches was to begin.

The fighting broke out in the plastic mine. As they had hoped, the ants overpowered the roach warriors who stood guard over them, but one roach slipped away and alerted others. The ants in the mine soon found themselves surrounded by warriors and their fellow ants in the colony, unaware of the situation, did not come to their aid.

Roach warriors put down the revolt with astonishing speed and ruthlessness. As if killing the rebel ants were not enough, the roaches broke into the homes of the ants they had killed. Any larva found in these homes were carried to the surface and left in the sun along with the bodies of the rebels.

It was a terrible punishment since the entire colony was forced to watch for several h-units as larva of various ages squeaked in agony and died from excessive exposure to the sun and dehydration.

The ants were not permitted to cover any of these dead. Those who herded the grasshoppers reported that swarms of flies laid their eggs upon the carcasses. Roach warriors were delighted since they considered fly eggs a delicacy—an expensive one.

Following this tragedy, the Colony Council was forced to disband. Council Chief Delana was placed under guard in her domicile and allowed no visitors. More warriors arrived to patrol the tunnels, seizing ants at random for the least infraction and tossing them into the mantis pit. All colony training centers for young adults were closed. Parents had to teach their young adults to read and write after twelve-h-unit work days, which they often had no energy to do. Later, Delana was assigned to work with the refuse collectors.

Delana did not seem to find this demeaning, as the roaches thought she would, but worked alongside her fellow colony members as cheerfully as possible. Secret communications resumed with a double system, to be sure everyone got every message.

Through all this, Rashad left Master Daeira alone. A warrior watched her every move outside her domicile, and Rashad dropped in at random, uninvited. He often had to wait an h-unit or more before she came out of her meditative trance. He questioned her at length, every time, but she said as little as possible to him. She, too, worked over half of each day with her fellow colony members, mostly taking the job of water-carrier. Like Delana, she managed to be encouraging, even though she was no longer allowed to speak to colony members on Seventhdays. Public meditation had been suspended.

At the beginning of Twelfth Time Frame, Master Daeira had the most wonderful dream-vision of her life. The vision was so overwhelming that, at first, she could not describe it accurately.

"Essence," she said over and over in her thoughts, even while carrying water jars, "I cannot put into words what you have shown me. Please, grant me the words I need to share this glorious vision."

Every night, she would stay up an extra h-unit attempting to write down for others what she had seen on that incredible journey through the history of their planet. Essence answered her request and provided the words she needed.

Rashad's "visit" interrupted one of these writing sessions.

"Well, at least you are awake," was his first comment.

Daeira closed her journal. "What may I do for you this night?" she asked.

"I thought you would like to know that I am going to let you have your Last Day ritual. But there will be warriors in attendance, and even if they can't understand what you say, I can."

"And if I say something you don't like?"

"You know what will happen."

Part of Master Daeira did not care what happened to her, but if she were tossed into the mantis pit, the colony would no longer have her guidance to live through this trial that never seemed to end—another matter for her to meditate upon.

"Will Sir Ragnar be attending?" Master Daeira asked because Rashad had mentioned that he might visit the colony again.

"He has more important things to do, but I'm sure Warrior Commander Rand will be with me." Rashad knew those "important things" would be the Last Night party Sir Ragnar always held in Roacheria for fellow Board Members. Rashad and the warriors would celebrate in the ant colony, too, and many of them would probably be ill the following morning due to over-consumption of ale. Ragnar had actually shipped a huge supply to his warriors, but with the instructions that half of them had to be on duty First Day. They would get to have their party the next evening.

Master Daeira nodded. "Is there anything else? I must meditate upon what I will say during services that day."

"Not at the moment."

As soon as Rashad left, Master Daeira began to write with a passion she had never known before.

By the time Last Day arrived, Daeira had written down all she would say, so she could repeat it to each group of discouraged colony members.

"My fellow ants," she began, "Essence has given me a vision of hope to share with you. I know each one of you will take from it what meaning you will and apply it to your lives while we live under others' control. We are the ones who must show all our compassion, in spite of everything. We are the example of Essence. We are all Her voice, Her eyes, Her pods, in this world. We must trust, now more than ever, that She will bring into our hearts what we need each h-unit of every day."

Then she related her dream:

In the beginning, Essence roamed the skies looking for the right place to start a world. She saw that our planet already had cycles of day and night, water and air. It had a set path around its sun so its cycles could be numbered, but it had no life.

"I will see what can live and grow here," she said, and joined herself with it. The Creative Life Force of Essence endowed the waters with miniscule plants and creatures and the cycle of life began. Essence cherished this new life, but was tired from her journey across the cosmos, so she entered the earth and went to sleep.

Eons later, when she awoke, the planet was filled with life forms. The water and land and air teemed with a great variety of plants and creatures. Some were tiny and frail, others huge and fierce. There was great variety even in their coverings—smooth, hard, scaly, furry. The large, scaly ones dominated at that time.

Essence watched her world. The sun fed the plants, which fed the moving creatures, who then were eaten by larger ones, and on and on. They grew, propagated, and returned to feed the earth when their time was over. Some creatures failed and disappeared, but new ones evolved to take their place.

And ants were there.

Essence, satisfied with the balance and cycles, cradled her world, and went to sleep again.

The pain of many shocks woke Essence. Chunks of matter hurled through the cosmos and struck the planet, killing millions of life forms and knocking the planet in its cosmic path. The dust from their impact screened the sun's light, denying life-giving energy to plants. Essence watched in dismay as thousands of species disappeared from her cherished world. In her grief, she shook. Hills tumbled. Mountains sent forth liquid fire from within.

But even in grief, Essence's Creative Life Force found its way again. An infinite variety of flowering plants came to be. A few species

of the scaly creatures and the small ones with fur and feathers survived.
And ants were still there.

Essence watched for many eons as the fur creatures increased in size and began to dominate. "What would happen," Essence said, "if I interfered and gave one life form an advantage? If I gave a tad of my intelligence to a creature, could it create something original, as I have?"

Essence looked closely at each species and finally chose one that seemed different from others. This species was not entirely covered with fur, stood on only two appendages, and had a well-developed nervous system. She infused them with more intelligence and waited to see what would happen.

Season cycles passed. Generations of Duo Pods came and went. Essence saw that they made tools, built things, and developed the planet. Their machines grew ever more complex. Satisfied, Essence took a nap.

Essence awoke with a fever. The planet's surface was a shambles. The air and the water were fouled. All the Duo Pods, all of the feathered creatures, and most of the furry ones were dead forever.

"What has happened to my world?" Essence cried.

Grief for her failed experiment and illness consumed Essence. The earth shook. Storms raged. Her tears covered many lands. Then slowly, the earth healed itself. Although it would take many more eons for all of the Duo Pod creations to return to the earth, the world looked new and fresh once more. Essence found that one substance the Duo Pods had made would not break itself down and feed the earth. They had indeed created something original. Her experiment had not been a total failure.

She looked around hopefully and found that ants, roaches and other insects were not only still there, but had grown greatly in size and changed in other ways.

"Ah, my faithful ants," she said. "You have been with me from the earliest days and have always been civilized. Perhaps the intelligence I gave the Duo Pods was not enough. I will try again. I will give you not only the gift of knowledge, but my compassion as well. And this

time, I will not sleep, but will watch over my world. I will be available to my creatures, speaking to their minds when they seek me. When each one's time on earth is done, the part of me that is in them will return to me in unity forever. Eat then, my ants, of the lasting creation of the Duo Pods—plastic—and receive my gifts. Cherish my world and seek to understand its mysteries."

And so we are.

While Essence was speaking, a group of roaches approached. They took the gift of intelligence, but ran away before the second, more important gift of compassion and inner essence was given. Thus they received no more of Essence than had the extinct Duo Pods.

Bemused, Essence observed the roaches as they ran from her. "I must watch and see what comes of this development."

Master Daeira stood silently when she finished relating the dream-message. The meditation chamber was silent as well. The ants meditated longer than they ever had before on the events of that season cycle and how they needed to live their lives in the days and season cycles to come.

Thankfully, Rashad remained silent, too, and he led Rand out of the chamber before the sharing of honeydew, although the warriors remained. Rand told the warriors to refuse if offered the cups of honeydew. Rashad and Rand did not return for the other sessions—which Rashad explained to the warrior commander would be exactly the same as the one he had witnessed.

"What was all that about? What did she tell them?" Rand asked afterward in Rashad's domicile.

Rashad explained the meaning of the creed, the lighting of the beeswax lamps, the sharing of the cups of honeydew, and the general idea of Last Day.

"And that long talk of hers that silenced them for so long?"

Rashad said only, "It was a long story—hard for me to follow—but harmless to us."

"Get a copy of that parchment she read from and translate it fully!"

Rashad bowed and swept his front pods outward.

He waited until late in the evening to enter Master Daeira's domicile.

"Commander Rand wants a copy of what you said today," he demanded, putting out his pod to take it. "I need to translate if for him. I found your statement that we have no essence to be insulting!"

Master Daeira said, "I said what I said, that which Essence revealed to me. Have you roaches demonstrated any evidence that you have the compassion of Essence?" She handed him a piece of parchment, for she had anticipated this request. Many copies had already gone out through the covered hole in the wall, located behind a curtain in her sanitation area, to her neighboring domicile. Rashad took the parchment in silence and glanced over it. If he noticed that his copy lacked the last two paragraphs, and ended with "And so we are," he said nothing.

After reading the translation, Rand crumpled it up and threw it on Rashad's floor. Rashad carefully flattened it out and put it inside his journal.

13.

Last Day, 16 B.C.C.

Dart fed his son a carefully measured portion of ground plastic mixed with honeydew while Dodie prepared their Last Day meal. "What did you think about Master Daeira's vision?" she asked.

"I was confused by it at first. Strange, but I was angry and peaceful at the same time. But when we finished meditating, I began to think that she is right. Maybe roaches can learn compassion if we demonstrate it to them. Maybe Rashad will be able to change their minds to allow us plastic again. I don't know. I just feel more hopeful than I have in a long time."

"I do, too, although I don't know why."

Seventh Time Frame
13, 15 B.C.C.

Winter turned to spring and then summer. Sir Ragnar arrived shortly before Summer Solstice. Finding the colony running smoothly with no violence or rebellion, all ants bowing before him in total respect, he recalled some of his warriors, although Rashad overheard him tell Rand to keep a careful eye on everything.

"Sir," Rashad was bold enough to say, "Ever since the ants celebrated their Last Day ritual, they have been much more complacent. Will you allow them to have their Summer Solstice celebration?"

Sir Ragnar looked at him curiously. "What do they do?"

"They roast whole grasshoppers—it is delicious, Sir—and they sing and dance. It's tomorrow. Why not stay and see?"

Sir Ragnar twitched his antennae. "Why not?"

It was the closest the ants had come to happiness since before Sir Ragnar's first horrific visit. Although nervous, a group of ants performed their traditional songs and dances before Sir Ragnar. He seemed impressed—stomping his pods in rhythm upon the ground in front of him. He asked Rashad many questions about what was going on, and Rashad answered at length. "Curious creatures," he said to Rashad at one point. "Stupid, but they do work hard now that they are properly subjugated."

Delana served Sir Ragnar herself, stooping in low humility to hand him a bowl of roasted grasshopper covered in honeydew sauce.

Master Daeira handed him a mug of fermented honeydew. "Thank you for allowing us this time of celebration. Rashad, would you kindly ask if we may return to having Seventhdays for rest and meditation?"

Rashad turned to his powerful employer and made the humble request.

Sir Ragnar chewed thoughtfully on the tender roast grasshopper, slid a pod sticky with sauce into and out of his mouth—cleaning it—gulped the honeydew, and finally said, "I suppose so, as long as they work an extra half an h-unit each day the other six days. Oh, and make sure four large jugs of this delicious beverage are shipped to me every time frame along with the hoppers you've been sending."

Rashad repeated the response in Ant. Daeira and Delana backed away slowly, saying, "Thank you," over and over.

"One thing at a time," Daeira said to Delana later. "Perhaps by this season cycle's Last Day, we shall have plastic back."

But Last Day came and went without a visit from Sir Ragnar.

Second Time Frame, 14 B.C.C.

Rashad began to visit Master Daeira on a regular schedule, rather than barging in without notice. He asked questions politely and Daeira answered in more depth than she had for a while, hoping she might yet influence him in ant ways so they could receive their plastic rations once again.

"May I ask," he said one evening, "how does an ant father choose a name for his young?"

"It is not the father who chooses, but the mother, or the two of them together. Often, the first-hatched is named for the mother; many names have male and female versions. A mother might also name her larva after a family member who has died, or one whom she admires very much. Names can come from either the mother or the father's side of the family or from the colony members as a whole."

"Admired very much...is that why I hear the name Daeira used so much lately?"

Daeira nodded. "I feel honored that many have chosen to name their female young after me." In her mind, she said, I just wish there were not so many young ones hatching out. Essence, help us.

After several such conversations, Daeira broached the subject of plastic. "Rashad, you know our young will suffer and die of plastic depravation. Please, could you ask Sir Ragnar to restore our portions?"

Rashad shifted uneasily. "I will propose it, but he may not grant it."

After Sir Ragnar's next visit, during which plastic for the ants was not restored, Rashad asked Daeira, "Why have there been no mating ceremonies lately?"

Master Daeira gave him a long look and was silent for a full moment before saying, "It is a serious moral wrong for us to mate when we cannot feed our young properly. Since you will not allow us plastic for our young, adult males and females of mating age remain single."

"Do they not desire each other?"

"Of course they desire each other! But they cherish each other, and their possible future young, enough not to mate when they can't feed their young necessary plastic. We do not willfully make our young suffer."

Both were silent for a few moments. Daeira hoped that he remembered so long ago when she had explained the word "cherish" to a much younger Rashad. He had said there was no such word in Roach.

Master Daeira pleaded with Rashad. "Please, can you convince him to allow us plastic?"

"We'll see," was the only answer she got.

First Time Frame, 13 B.C.C.

The following winter, a couple of desperate parents tried to take some plastic from the mine in the satchels they used for their mid-day meal. It wasn't so much for the plastic as it was to make a statement to the roaches. One of the warriors saw the bulging bag. He snatched it from the back of the female ant and opened it.

Angry words that the ants could not understand followed, and the pair was dragged before Rand. Rashad was summoned to interpret.

"Why are you stealing plastic?" Rashad asked them.

The ants looked at Rashad and said, "How can we be stealing what is rightfully ours to begin with?"

"Who told you to do this?" Rashad demanded.

"No one. We did it on our own, for our young one."

Rashad spoke to Rand in roach as the two ants hung their heads. As expected, they were hauled off to the mantis pit. They did not fight or cry out. Neither did they beg for mercy.

The roaches found nothing when they ransacked the pair's domicile looking for a larva to leave in the sun.

Later, word went through the secret communications system that during the few days before, they had passed all their hidden plastic to a neighbor. That morning, the neighbor had taken their only larva into her home.

An edict went out from Rand that no mine worker could carry a satchel into the mine. All workers left their mid-day meals at the entrance and went there to eat, leaving the empty sacks there when they finished.

Fourth Time Frame, 10 B.C.C.

Young adults who emerged from pupation the first three season cycles of no plastic portions were still intelligent because they had entered their pupate state before the loss of plastic.

Duncan fell into his pupate sleep one morning the following spring. His parents carefully prepared their hidden plastic into the finely ground mixture of plastic and honeydew that he would consume during his pupate sleep. Pupas did not need as great an amount as that which a larva received, but they still needed some plastic. Dart and Dodie lined up the seven jugs of the mixture next to the floor cushion upon which Duncan would sleep for the next seven season cycles. The jugs stood on pedestals of decreasing heights. Tubes made of hollow reeds went from one jug to the next, lower and lower, and then to Duncan's mouth. The end of the tube was secured inside his mouth with soft strands of woven thistledown. The plastic mixture would trickle down slowly, a few drops a day, one jar per season cycle.

Dart and Dodie caressed their sleeping young one and secured the portal to that chamber. Then they passed the last of their hidden supply through the hole between their domicile and the next so that some other young might get enough.

"Duncan will be very important in this colony one day," Dodie said.

"We can hope that, of course, but what makes you seem so certain," Dart replied.

"I don't know. Just a feeling. May Essence grant that he emerge in happier times."

The two rested their abdomens on the floor and lifted their front pods in meditation. "Essence, Author of Life, Giver of Compassion, Solace of our Hearts, Ultimate Provider, let Duncan sleep soundly and undisturbed. May his metamorphosis turn him into an intelligent and compassionate adult. Call him to whatever purpose you wish for him. We give him to your care. Deliver us from this time of trial and free us somehow from slavery to these roaches. Send the answer to our plea to your mouth piece, Master Daeira, in her dreams. Protect her from the anger of Sir Ragnar. Be with us all. As you wish."

14.

Thirteenth Time Frame, 295 C.C.I., Henry Roach-Dairier II

To: Henry Roach-Dairier II
        Fire Ant 2
        Combined Colonies of Insectia
From: Gabrielle Roach
        Meadow Commonwealth
        Roacheria

My Most Cherished Son:

I expected some problems with Sir Rastus when applying for an archaeological dig on his surface area, but not quite to this degree. Yesterday, he arrived in my SERCB work chamber with an enforcer. I have to admit, the enforcer looked almost apologetic when he served me with official papers.

"I know that son of yours is not in Roacheria right now, but you'd better get him back here from wherever he is! I've had these papers served to you since I assume you'll be defending him."

"Defending him from what?" I asked.

"From slandering my good family name, of course! Let's see your piddling family come up with this amount!"

I decided it would be best not to say anything more, so I simply took the papers of the suit against you. I read the allegations carefully—three times. He claims that the work you are doing, and the proposed archeological dig, are for the sole purpose of ruining his family name throughout all Roachstory and (supposedly) far into the future. He's demanding huge damages, and of course, denying permission for the dig.

Rastus must have some connections with the Chief Enforcer as to the timing of his suit because he's got the hearing scheduled right in the middle of four other cases I have at the moment giving me very little time to prepare.

However, I do not want you to worry. He hasn't a pod to stand on, legally speaking. And even if he wins because he's influenced the Chief Enforcer, we have so many friends here and in the colonies (of whom he knows nothing) who would gladly provide his monetary demand. While the amount is staggering, if everyone who supports us each gave a 100th_ part coin, there would be more than enough.

I'm sorry to say I searched your sleep chamber here looking for those letters that you wrote to him that were returned unopened. They will serve as proof of your good intentions and his refusal to see you. I didn't find them. If you have them with you in Fire 1, please send them to me immediately. If not, tell me where to look at Meadow Commonwealth. Also, please return a few days ahead of the hearing date, the 13th of this time frame, because I will need to prepare you for the interrogation you'll endure from Sir Rastus' counselor.

Your cherishing mother,
Gabrielle

To: *Gabrielle Roach*
        Meadow Commonwealth
        Roacheria
From: *Henry Roach-Dairier II*

Cherished Mother:

I am not as surprised as you were at Sir Rastus' actions. In fact, I hid those letters very carefully, thinking that he might send enforcers with search permission to find them or hire bandits to attack Meadow Commonwealth seeking to destroy them. The messenger bearing this letter will show you where they are.

> *Your devoted son,*
> *Henry*

It was actually the library curator who had cautioned me to hide those letters because they could become legal documents. Worried that a written message might be intercepted, I kept my letter intentionally vague, but the trusted messenger knew he needed to clear out the main compartment of the writing surface in my sleep chamber. In the front-right corner was a tiny gap—enough for the tip of a pod to pry up the false bottom of the compartment. Beneath that piece of wood were all the letters I had written to Sir Rastus asking to hear his family's "side" of the story, including the ones that had been returned unopened.

After sending the messenger with the letter, I explained to my friends in Fire 2 that I would have to leave in a few days. (I had pretty much completed my work there anyway.)Fire 2's archivist looked at the amount and my mother's statement about 100th-part coins. "We may not have Roacherian coins lying around in an ant colony, but why do so many roaches still forget they are not dealing with an individual when they take action against an ant?"

I found it both amusing and reassuring to be referred to as an "ant."

"Those who do not truly understand our ways are too wrapped up in themselves to realize we are all part of a larger community." I replied. "They also think that because I am a Roacherian citizen I am alone in what I do. They forget that Meadow Commonwealth is much more an extension of the Combined Colonies than it is a Roacherian community. None the less, I have to go and answer this before the Chief Enforcer."

As I walked the trail back to Meadow Commonwealth, I thought about the evolution of thought among ants concerning the belief that roaches have no essence. Master Daeira's words to her community concerning many roaches lack of compassion, and therefore lack of essence, was understandable in her time and circumstances. However, that literal interpretation contributed to the hostility between ants and roaches more than it should have.

It had taken the courage of ants like Master Anthony and Master Henrietta, who adopted a roach nymph, to begin to see that the words, "I will be available to my creatures, speaking to their minds when they seek me," referred to roaches as well as ants. The story of our creation was meant to be interpreted symbolically, not literally. My grandfather told me time and again—as his father and grandfather had told him—it was more a matter of roaches not seeking Essence's guidance than not having her presence within them.

Essence could not be present in every leaf, twig, or rock and not be in roaches as well. It took many ants, and roaches like my grandfather, having visions long after South Dairy 1 was freed to see the deeper meaning of the vision Essence gave Master Daeira of the planet's history. But it had come as a vision of hope in time of trial, when it certainly seemed as though roaches had no essence. We must seek Essence if we are to find Her within ourselves. It has only been since 202 C.C.I., when my antcestor Henry Harvester and his companions Howard and Herbert returned from their imprisonment in the pods of Sir Rex, that ants began to think beyond the literal meaning of: "no more essence than had the extinct duo pods."

Master Henrietta's father—the first Henry of my antcestors—set the example for one roach, Gabriel—my mother's name sake. He followed that example and sought Essence. If Henry hadn't set the example, if Gabriel had not listened and worked to set Henry and his companions free all those season cycles ago, if my great-great-grandfather Anthony and his mate Henrietta had not adopted a roach egg—my great-grandfather—we might still be locked in that place of hatred. There are still a few ants who don't like to admit it, but ant hatred toward roaches has existed, too.

Would I be able to convince Sir Rastus, and if not him at least the Chief Enforcer, that my purpose was to continue the healing, not widen the division again?

Fourth Time Frame, 3 B.C.C.

For the next several season cycles, life with no plastic went on in South Dairy 1. The ants carefully used and shared the plastic they had hidden. As time went by, they stretched it out with a little less each day to every larva. In her private journal in the spring of 8 B.C.C., Master Daeira wrote:

> *I know Essence is with us. But she is so silent of late. No dreams at all. Our communication network reports that plastic is running dangerously short for our young. Those now emerging are still healthy and intelligent because they entered pupation when we had enough. But how much is "enough"? Can we actually do with less? Is this what Essence wants to show us, but we never would have reduced the amounts unless forced to as we are now? It has been hard for me to keep up the faith of the entire colony of late. I feel so very inadequate.*

Duncan emerged from pupation right on schedule. His mother had stayed home for a few days to be sure she was there when he opened his chamber door. He was only bewildered for a moment or two as he sheltered his eyes to the dim light of the bees' wax lamp. His mother embraced him immediately.

"Welcome, my wonderful son," she said. "We have long waited for you to emerge as an adult."

Duncan felt her pods stroking him all over and mimicked her movements. His first words were, "I know you." They spent the rest of the day talking, and Dodie explained as much as she could about life in their colony.

More embraces came when Dart returned from herding the grasshoppers for the day. "You look so much like my father," Dart told his son. "I wish you could have been able to meet him." This was followed by an explanation of death while they ate dinner.

Rashad still allowed parents one day to bond with their new adult young—mainly so those new adults would know what was expected of them. Dart hung his head as he said to his son, "We are slaves to these roaches. You are so lucky to be healthy and intelligent! We fed you plastic that we had saved and hidden before the roaches denied us all plastic. I'm sorry to have to tell you that you have come into such a terrible time in our colony's antstory. All colony members used up the last of the supplies we had hidden five season cycles ago. No young have had any since then."

"Dart," Dodie interrupted, "we can explain more of that later. Tomorrow, we will go to the Heart of the Colony and show him where his grandparents feed the earth. We will explain the rest as we show him everything."

Both parents tried to be as cheerful as they could on that tour of their sad colony. "So I will work with one of you beginning tomorrow?" Duncan asked.

"Yes," his mother answered. "We will also teach you how to read and write a little each evening, when we are all not too tired. We felt that since you can't learn as we did, in a training center with other young adults, that we would have you spend half a time frame with each of us. You can go with your father tomorrow and begin to learn about his job on the surface. Then you can spend time with me as I carry messages all over the colony. Then you may decide which job you like better."

Their last stop before returning home was to introduce Duncan to Master Daeira, who still liked to meet each new adult, especially since there were fewer and fewer of them these days. She took both his front pods in hers and held them for quite some time, looking deeply into his eyes. "There is something special about you. I feel it. I see it in your eyes. Essence has a plan for you that will soon be revealed."

Dodie looked at Dart in a way that said, "I knew it."

Most of the season cycle, those who herded the grasshoppers stayed on the surface with them day and night. For his first quarter time frame, Duncan learned about day duty with his father. Dart's fellow dairying ants congratulated him on the emergence of an intelligent young adult. They had been stretched to the limit in protecting the hoppers with half as many workers as there had been a generation earlier.

Duncan caught on quickly to helping his father watch from the edge of the pasture area, keeping a wary eye on the hopper nymphs who often bounded off into higher grass where predators might be hidden. "Those roaches are just standing around. Why don't they help?" Duncan asked.

"They only care that we don't try to run off," his father explained. "They are pretty good at hunting the mantis, but only because they want their share of grasshopper meat. They know if the mantises kill too many, they will be hungry, too."

The next quarter time frame, Dart was on night duty. Duncan looked in wonder at the night sky. It was a new moon and clear night, so Dart taught his son the names of a few star groups and how to find the way back to the colony in darkness without using the trail from the pasture to the main colony entrance.

"Why don't we just fight off these roaches?" Duncan asked.

Dart told him about what happened when they tried. "It is wrong to throw away one's life foolishly," he concluded.

"What if someone snuck away in the night? Aren't there more ants like us somewhere who would help?"

"Yes. There is a colony of dairying ants about a day-long journey from here. Long ago, our antcestors came from that colony and began this one. But those roach warriors have sharp senses, even in the darkness. Sometimes their night senses seem to be better than ours. Stay here. Watch what happens when I try to move too far away."

Duncan watched as Dart moved off a little way from the herd of hoppers. Instantly, a warrior appeared in front of Dart, mandibles open wide, hissing at him, pointing back to the hopper herd. Dart pointed to his abdomen—a signal that he needed to relieve himself of body waste. The warrior grunted and stayed with Dart as he went to the surface latrine behind some tall grass.

"See what I mean?" Dart told his son when he returned. "If I had run, or if I had tried to go beyond the latrine, I would be dead right now, and you would have no father. It has happened too many times. Don't tempt them. They kill us for no reason."

Duncan asked no more questions that night.

Seventhday came and the family rested. This was Duncan's second time listening to Master Daeira explain to groups of colony members that Essence had not abandoned them. She was waiting for the "right time". Daeira spent extra time with a group of young adults, all in their first two years of adulthood, teaching them to meditate. She looked intently at each young male and female, but her eyes seemed to settle on Duncan more than the others, as if searching for the answer to an unasked question. Duncan returned her steady gaze, understanding that many things were said to each other without words because that roach Rashad was always present for these teaching sessions. Duncan had been told many times already to be careful what he said within Rashad's sensitive hearing.

Duncan tried to explain his feelings to his mother that evening. Dart had already gone to sleep because he had to go back to day duty. Duncan would be following his mother around the colony tomorrow. "Does everyone have strange feelings during meditation?"

"What do you mean?" Dodie asked.

"Well, last Seventhday and this, I felt such a strange mixture of good feelings and fear."

"What makes you fearful?"

"The roaches."

"They make us all feel fearful. What else seems strange to you?"

"It's hard to find the right words. When I lift my pods like Master Daeira showed us, and begin to form words in my mind to Essence, I get this very strange feeling. It's not fear, not joy, not exactly peace, but…I don't know. It's like straining for the sound of a predator moving at night, and then the relief of knowing there isn't one. I know that doesn't make sense."

"Take my pod in yours and let us meditate together. Perhaps the feeling will come again and you'll be able to put words to it."

Mother and son joined their uplifted pods in silence. Then Dodie spoke her meditation. "Essence, are you trying to speak to my son? If you are, please allow him the most peaceful feeling of all so that his mind will quiet itself to hear Your voice."

The two of them sat that way for several moments. Finally, they lowered their pods. Duncan looked at his mother. He could tell she was waiting for him to say something. "I felt very content, as if somehow all the bad with the roaches will go away. But how could that happen?"

Dodie took his pods in hers again. "Keep your mind and your heart open. Pay attention to your dreams. When we are out delivering messages tomorrow, we shall stop and see Master Daeira again—she is on my delivery route—and perhaps she can help you understand."

Master Daeira was pleased to see Duncan and his mother the following day. She took Duncan's pods in hers. "I had a dream about you last night. I believe more than ever that Essence has a special purpose for you."

"I have long felt that way," Dodie said.

Duncan looked at the earthen floor. All this fuss over him—it was confusing and unsettling to say the least. His night had been dreamless.

"Duncan, you don't have to feel awkward with me."

He looked up at Master Daeira. How had she sensed his feelings?

"I know how it is to feel that much is expected of you and you don't even know what the task is, let alone how to accomplish it. All I ask is that you keep your mind and heart open. Can you do that?"

Duncan nodded.

Master Daeira turned to Dodie. "If at all possible, Duncan must work with you, rather than your mate. He must be able to come here whenever he needs to for guidance." She turned to Duncan and took his pods again. "I have many nights when I dream nothing. But then of a sudden, something comes to me. I would not want that to happen when you are out on the surface—not that your father's work is unimportant—but you would not be free to seek me out at any time. Is that all right with you?"

Duncan lifted his front pods in affirmation but was thinking, I don't know. I suppose so.

Both females stroked him gently. Duncan's breathing, which had been short and quick, turned to long, relaxed breaths. He smiled for the first time since his first day of adulthood.

Days passed into time frames. Duncan learned his way around even the tiniest of colony tunnels. He knew the name of everyone along his mother's messenger route. Then she turned him over to other messengers, one by one, until he knew every route in the colony— even better than Dodie did. His intelligence amazed everyone he met. His presence gave many colony members hope that Essence would grant their young what was needed without actually having plastic. His dreams were fuzzy, cloud-like lands of contentment.

The inevitable happened. Young adults with "mild" plastic deprivation began to emerge. They could be taught the easy tasks about the colony—hauling water or diggings from the plastic mine, taking away refuse, and all things that required only a strong thorax and the ability to plod along behind someone else, but they talked little. Reading and numbers were beyond their ability to comprehend.

As the ants searched for ways to help these young adults know the dignity of some kind of work, they began to ask themselves what would come next. By the time Duncan turned seventeen, emerging adults had more and more problems. Sometimes their exoskeletons were too weak to carry any burden. Others became ill with the simplest infection and did not recover.

The plastic deprivation grew worse. Young adults emerged from pupation horribly deformed, died within a few days, or never emerged from pupation. The grief of the colony grew exponentially. Their young had reached a degree of plastic deprivation the ants had never seen.

Many colony members grew angry in their grief, wanting to rise up against their overseers even if they died for it.

Duncan woke with a start. He knew what they needed to do. He was ready to run out of their domicile, but his father—on day duty and home for the night—heard him and stopped him. Dart had to hush his son's excitement. Roach warriors patrolled the tunnels at night, listening for any possibility of revolt.

"Quiet down, Duncan. What is it?"

"I've got to go to Master Daeira! She, Essence, told me to go and get help. I could see it—I could see me on a journey to get help from that colony you told me about."

"Slow down, son. Tell me all, and then go to her at the start of the work-day. If they find you out and about at this hour, you won't live to see her."

Duncan lowered himself to the floor and sighed. His father fixed him some tea. Dodie joined them. "Start at the beginning," she said.

"It was night. I saw myself slipping away from our colony. But not by the main entrance. I was in the thick wood plants on the back side. I'm not sure how I got there. I knew by the stars which way to go, but I don't know the stars that well. I could not see anyone about, but a soft female voice said, 'Soon it will be the time for you to go and get help.' I also saw many different kinds of ants together. Then I woke up."

None of them could sleep after that. It was a long, difficult wait for the h-units to pass until the work-day began. Duncan left the moment he could and practically ran to the message center. He picked up his stack for the day, shuffled through it, put Master Daeira's on top, and nearly tripped over a roach warrior on his way out.

"Oh, I'm so sorry," he blurted out, lowering himself right to the dirt of the tunnel.

The warrior hissed at him and went on his way. Duncan got up, picked the messages, and forced himself to slow down.

Master Daeira's portal opened before he had a chance to knock.

"Come in," she whispered.

He closed her portal behind him, took the cup of tea she held out, and told her his dream.

"I know how you came to be in those wood plants," she said. "It is time. This is your purpose. But you must be quiet about it, and be patient. There is much to do before you get to those wood plants."

15.

Fall, 3 B.C.C.

On a crisp autumn day, roach traders arrived at what would later be named South Harvester Colony 45. The colony was about half a day's journey from a slow-moving, steep-banked river. The city of Roacheria lay a few h-units journey east of that river and was the location of the South Roach Control Board—the governing body over all roach surface area west of the Great River.

Not aggressive, these traders laid out several items on the ground about 100 f-units from the colony's main entrance and waited for the ants to come to them. They did not have an interpreter with them and could only gesture to the items and point to those around them.

A small group of ants came from within the colony to see what they wanted. Two of the roaches pantomimed the idea of trading. One roach put down a carton, removed one item from it, and held it out to the other. The second handed the first a small carton of raw plastic. The first then gave the item to the second. They looked at the ants in a questioning way, pointing to the items and to the ants.

The ants got the idea. They had been trading some of their plastic for honeydew and grasshopper meat with a nearby dairying colony for a couple of season cycles already.

One ant held up a pod as if to say, "Wait a moment." They needed to summon their council chief.

The roaches nodded their antennae and gestured toward their goods, inviting the ants to see what they offered. Several carrying baskets they had used to bring the trade goods sat behind piles of folded white cloths, pottery, jugs, utensils, some sort of tool to lift heavy objects—or at least that's what the ants thought it might be—, and other things the ants did not recognize.

The first roach picked up what looked like an insect's wing from a pile of them. He gestured and said, "Bzz," pantomimed cooking it, and then ate it. He handed some to the ants to taste. The ants soon figured out that somehow the roaches had captured many bees and then fried the wings. The strange food was crunchy and good tasting, so this might be a possible trade. (Later, they decided that if they all wanted some, they would figure out how to capture large numbers of bees themselves—although the idea of honey was more appealing than killing the bees for their wings.)

They had no need to trade for the pottery, jugs, or utensils since they produced those things themselves. They were much stronger than the roaches and could lift heavy burdens without the help of a machine, so there was no need for that contraption, either.

One of the ants picked up a piece of the cloth—something they did not have—and raised his pod in a questioning gesture. The second roach took another cloth, unfolded it, and using an unopened carton as a dining surface, demonstrated its use as a covering for a flat surface upon which to serve food.

"Oh," the ants said and nodded.

By that time, Council Chief Hesper, had arrived. "What do they want?" she asked.

"They have these things here that they want to trade for our plastic," the ant who had eaten the bees' wings answered. He told Hesper about each item.

"I rather like these cloths. It would certainly keep food and utensils cleaner," Hesper said.

"That's what I was thinking, too. But can they be washed?" The ant took the cloth and pantomimed washing it. The two roaches nodded their antennae.

"But we would need one for every domicile. It would not be fair for some but not all to have one," Hesper said. She took a piece of parchment she had brought with her and an ink pot and wrote down the number of domiciles in the colony—5,000 at that time. Ants and roaches had developed the same numbering system, even though their languages were very different.

The roaches looked very pleased at the number. They scratched a number of weight units of plastic below the 5,000—a huge amount.

Hesper shook her antennae—it was too much at once. The other ants agreed and began to turn away.

The first roach put up a pod and said something. Then ants did not know what he meant, but they hesitated. Perhaps there was room for negotiation here. Back and forth the gesturing went until both sides understood that the roaches would bring 500 cloths at a time and the ants would give them the amount of plastic for that number. That was more manageable. In ten time frames, every family would have a lovely white cloth upon which to serve meals.

Hesper wrote her name on the parchment, and so did one of the roaches. The two traders packed up their goods and pointed to the crescent moon in the clear sky that day. He used his pods to show it grow full, shrink, and come back to the current crescent. Then he pointed at the cloths and indicated delivery at that stage of the moon in the next time frame.

"We will study how these things are made," Hesper said as they went back into the colony. "Then we can produce them ourselves for new families."

The first two deliveries went smoothly. A group of about twenty roaches carried baskets with twenty-five cloths in each basket. The ants brought out the required weight units of plastic and they traded. Hesper, the Colony Council, and the entire colony liked the idea that now they had two trading partners—the dairying ants and these roaches.

When the two traders arrived with the third set of 500 cloths, it was nearly sundown, so the ants gestured toward the colony entrance, inviting the group of roaches to come underground for the night. They led their guests to the Council Chamber, because it was large enough for the whole group, and carried in some fluff from the seed pods of a common surface plant. Piles of the fluff made comfortable places to sleep. The ants fed their roach guests a dinner of the roasted seeds from the grassfrond plants they grew along with some meat from grasshoppers they had obtained from the dairying colony. There were nods and smiles all around. Their guests left early the next morning with friendly waves of their front pods.

By the time of the ninth delivery, a group of ants had figured out that the cloths were made from the same fluff they had always spread on their floors for sleeping. It wasn't much of a jump from there to realizing how bits of the fluff had been twisted together into long, thin strings. Further study of the cloth revealed the structure of weaving. Another inventive ant discovered that a long string could be poked through tiny holes on the edges of the cloth, back and forth, to form the cloth into a sack.

Then that same ant filled the sack with loose fluff and closed the end to form a mat—much neater and more comfortable than spreading fluff on the floor of their sleep chambers each night and sweeping it up in the morning. The Colony Council began to make plans for a work crew to gather more of the seed pods at the proper season each year. Those who planted and harvested the grassfronds set about experimenting with how to grow more of that type of plant.

The ants took the final delivery from the roach traders and passed over the last of the agreed-upon plastic. They gestured their thanks to the roach traders, but indicated there wasn't anything else they wanted or needed. The roaches looked disappointed as they left.

Less than a quarter time frame later, Council Chief Hesper sat with the Colony Council discussing plans for the long-term production of the new product—weaving cloth into sacks for sleep mats.

Her Chief of Engineering said, "It will take about a season cycle to build enough looms to weave the cloth needed for the whole colony, but we think assigning the number of workers required will be worth it. Those who train young adults for various jobs told me many of their trainees are interested in learning this new line of work."

"Yes," the Chief of Agriculture added, "and many of those who tend the grassfronds say that planting and tending the fluff plants will give them something to do between planting and harvesting grassfronds."

Hesper nodded. "This will definitely help our colony continue to increase in population without any family being deprived of anything. All our lives will be—"

She was interrupted by a surface scout running into the Council Chamber shouting, "A huge mass of roach warriors is only a d-unit away! They will be here in no time! I don't know how they got past the eastern out-mound without being detected."

The colony defended itself as best it could from this surprise attack. Many harvester ants died that day, but the invading roaches did not begin a wholesale slaughter. Once the ants lowered themselves into positions of helplessness—indicating they surrendered—the roaches stopped attacking. They stood around Hesper and the council members—the last defense had been of the Council Chamber—hissing, with threatening looks upon their faces.

The smell of fear floated copiously from every ant's antennae. Roach antennae sensed it. They knew they had won.

A large roach with three metal disks hanging from chains about his head entered the Council Chamber and stared at Hesper. Behind him came the two roach traders. These two pantomimed to the ants that as long as they did what the roach warriors indicated, they would live.

The realization struck Hesper that she had unwittingly given these roaches all the information they needed to invade: the number of adult households in the colony with their order for cloths and the layout of their tunnels when they had invited the roaches to stay that one time. "The good we thought it was has been turned against us," she moaned.

But the two traders also indicated that the ants could go on living as they had. The roaches would take what plastic they wanted, but the lives of the ants, with the plastic that they needed, would go on as well—as long as they did not fight back.

The takeover of South Harvester 45 was complete: Ninth Time Frame 1, 2 B.C.C.

Information from Research During My Mentorship in South Harvester 45, in 292 C.C.I. Henry Roach-Dairier II

The members of South Harvester 45 never knew the name of the SRCB Board Member who claimed ownership of the colony. It was obvious that the traders worked for him and had set the whole thing up. One of the council members of South Harvester 45 at that time had the presence of mind to look carefully at the Board Member's features and, being a talented artist, she made a sketch, which I was able to see preserved in the colony archives. It did not resemble Sir Ragnar at all. Neither did it look like any portraits of other SRCB Members at that time—although portraits of all of them were not available.

The portrait did, however, remind me somewhat of images of Rex Roach located in New South Dairy 50. My great-great-grandfather had those images made. I tried to find portraits and images of Rex's family line, but I learned that much of what might have been in Rex's home was destroyed by the roach enforcers after he was found guilty of inciting war and crimes against the colonies back in 219-221 C.C.I. While I, and others, might speculate whether or not Rex's clan was involved all those season cycles ago, nothing can be proven one way or the other.

16.

Eighth Time Frame, 2 B.C.C.

Duncan delivered Master Daeira's messages each day and stayed as long as he could.

"I'd like you to put me at the very end of your route," she said. "That way, I can teach you the things you need to be ready for the future. Otherwise, make your route completely different every day."

Duncan drained his mug of tea. "Why?"

"We don't want Rashad to know where to find you at any particular time of the day. For now, he'll figure out that he can find you here at the end of the day, but that will change later."

At that moment, Rashad barged in. "Why are you two meeting every day?" he demanded.

Master Daeira shot Duncan a look that he understood to mean, Be quiet and play along. His mentor remained calm. "Duncan is learning deep meditation from me," she answered simply. "Would you care to join us?"

Master Daeira got up from the dining surface and reclined on a floor cushion. Duncan moved two other floor cushions near her and plopped down on one of them, gesturing to the third for Rashad.

The two of them raised their front pods and closed their eyes. Master Daeira began. "You know the surface, Duncan, so picture yourself in the grove of the wood plants where the aphids suck sap. Feel the shade from the leaves upon your face. Open your mind."

Duncan did as instructed and remained perfectly quiet. They heard the portal slam as Rashad left.

Master Daeira stopped and rose quickly. "I take back what I said earlier about keeping me at the end. We will grab whatever time we can whenever we can. Now that he's gone, I know I can speak a bit more freely. What I am going to say must remain secret. Do you understand?"

Duncan nodded.

"The council has decided, through extensive conversations via the secret communication system, that a one-ant escape tunnel will be dug from inside the pottery storage chamber. That place was chosen because it is closest to the grove of wood plants in our dream. Once it is ready, you will leave through it three hours after darkness when the moon is new. Your father will be teaching you how to follow the stars to reach a dairying colony to the south-southwest of ours. I'll explain more another day. You'd better leave now. Rashad may be watching for you along a tunnel."

Duncan's mind reeled. "Me? Why? I know so little."

Master Daeira took his pods in hers, then stroked his antennae the way his mother did. "You will be ready for this by the time the tunnel is complete. Do not worry."

Duncan could only nod again as he left for home, still bewildered by what he had been asked to do.

"Did Master Daeira tell you?" Duncan's father asked after dinner.

"Some. She said you would teach me the stars." Duncan's dream had been beautiful, but making it a reality terrified him. He tried not to show it.

"We both will," his mother added, "beginning this evening. Let's meditate together first."

Dodie rose and pushed a piece of floor covering up against the portal. "That won't keep the roaches out, but it will give us warning."

Parents and son sat together on the floor, joined pods, and raised them. Each meditated silently. Duncan's was simple: What do you want me to do? I am so afraid. Why me? I didn't ask for this. No answer came, but a feeling of peace moved through him.

After their meditation, Dart told his son to lie on his back beside him. Dodie held over them a piece of black fabric with tiny white dots painted on it mounted in a tight frame. One by one, Dart named individual stars and groups of stars. Duncan remembered a few of them, but he had forgotten most of what he had learned about the night sky since he began working underground.

"You must memorize these exactly because this is what the sky will look like when you escape," his father said. "We will do this every night until you can point to each one when I ask you to. Then you will learn how the sky turns with the hours of the night. Once you know the night sky, I will begin to teach you what was taught to me about the land forms along the way to our sister colony. The trail no longer exists, so you must learn the way by the sky, the dark hills, and streams."

Duncan had to voice his fear. "What if I get lost?"

His father's pods circled him. "I firmly believe Essence will guide you."

The following morning, Duncan intentionally tripped and dropped all his messages. Then he scooped them up without straightening out the order again. The next day, he managed to bump into another messenger and scrambled their messages together. "Oh, well, it doesn't matter who delivers the message, does it?" he asked.

He reported both these strategies to Master Daeira. "Good ideas, but you won't be able to do that every day."

"I know. What else can I do?"

Daeira paced about her chamber. "Tomorrow, grab someone else's pile. I'll put out the word to your supervisor and she'll come up with something permanent."

Duncan's supervisor explained quietly to all the messengers. Every morning after that, each messenger—without looking at the recipients—tossed a few of their messages in Duncan's pile and pulled out the same number. The last ant to do so would stir Duncan's pile around. Duncan would try to be the last to arrive, or would take himself to the sanitation area before leaving the message center. In addition, Duncan would "re-sort" his pile so that sometimes he began with the one on the top and other days he would begin with the bottom one. All this made his day a bit longer because he often back-tracked to tunnels, domiciles, or workplaces he had already been, but it did make him hard to locate during the workday. He would stop at Master Daeira's domicile whenever he was nearby and stay as long as he dared.

"The tunnel to the wood plants is nearly half complete," Master Daeira told him two time frames later. "But you must wait until the nights are the longest—soon after the new season cycle begins. Your father will explain more. How are you coming with learning the night sky?"

"I know all the main star groups, but I get some of them mixed up. I would do better if I weren't so tired when I get home each evening."

Daeira nodded. "Wait one moment," she said and went to her writing surface, picked up an ink pot, and hastily wrote something down. "Take this to your parents. It tells how to concentrate honeydew. Consume the concentrated honeydew each day with your mid-day meal and you'll have more energy the rest of the day. But do not consume it past mid-day. You do need to sleep at night."

"Thank you." Duncan put the instructions in his personal satchel, rather than his messenger's satchel.

Later that evening, Dart said, "Son, it has been four generations since the last ant traveled from here to our sister dairying colony. This map, carefully preserved by the members of her family since then, is the most accurate we have. You must trust Essence to guide you when your memory fails. You will not be able to take this map with you when you go; it would be too dark to see it anyway."

The positions of the stars seemed to muddle in Duncan's mind with the sequence of known landmarks. Was it the narrow stream and then the wide one? Or the other way around? This angle to that star on the far edge of the wood plants? Or was it the wider angle to that other star? Would he ever get it right? Was that fire ant colony still between him and his goal? Would the scent marks that announced their boundaries really be there?

There were days Duncan wished he had never had that dream. It was a relief that it rained during the New Moon right after the tunnel was ready, postponing his escape until the New Moon of Second Time Frame.

Master Daeira came to his rescue. "Promise me you will meditate deeply before beginning each memorization session. You must trust Essence, and plan to go to the medical facility as soon as you can after your return. Your eyes tell me how tired you are."

"I will," Duncan promised. He did the deep meditation as well, and felt more confident for it. The New Moon came. The night was clear.

His mother handed him an even greater concentration of honeydew at supper. She had boiled it until it was solid and crunchy. "This will give you the stamina you need tonight."

Both parents caressed him before one of the tunnel builders, who had slipped silently from one back-tunnel to the next, away from patrolling roach warriors, came to get him.

Duncan followed his guide through several smaller tunnels in a roundabout route to the pottery storage chamber. At each corner, they stopped, checking for roach warriors who patrolled the colony after everyone was supposed to be in their domiciles for the night. Duncan had to clench his outer mandibles together to keep them from clicking in his anxiety.

"I've been checking each night," his guide whispered, "noting what time they patrol each area. They are so regular. Come this way, now."

They slipped quietly into the pottery storage area and went to the very back of the chamber. Duncan's guide lifted some brown fabric covered with smooth dirt. Duncan would never have known a hole lay behind it.

"I'll be here every night at this same time, checking for you. I've been coming every night for the last quarter time frame as it is. A few more nights will be easy. But your fellow messengers can only cover for you for so long. You must return as soon as possible."

"I will. Thank you."

"No, thank you! I firmly believe you will be successful. Essence be with you."

Duncan slipped into the narrow tunnel and his guide flapped the fabric back into place. Even the deep, relaxation breathing Master Daeira had taught him did not dispel his fear.

The total darkness did not concern Duncan—he had gotten used to it by feeling his way around his own sleep chamber after his parents had put out the last beeswax lamp. It was the strong earthy smell and the roughness of the narrow tunnel's walls, ceiling, and floor that was discomforting. He supposed the odor was because the earth was so freshly dug, compared to the tunnels of the colony. The low ceiling and roughness were likely because the tunnel's builders were in a hurry to complete it. Young adults emerged from pupation and died of plastic deprivation every week. They needed help as soon as possible. Even though no single adults had mated for many season cycles, eggs still hatched to others who had mated before the roaches deprived them of plastic.

This urgency pushed Duncan along the escape tunnel. It went along at the same level for quite some distance and then gradually slanted upward. Duncan had been told that a flap of sod covered the opening in the grove of wood plants. He would have to push up on it gently. There was supposed to be a slender seedling in the center of the flap to mark the place for his return. But how would he know what it looked like in the dark? How would he find it when he came back?

The smell of the soil changed as he neared the surface. He felt the flap, pushed it gently upward. Fresh air surrounded him. He let his antennae explore every direction for the scent of roaches before emerging from the hole. Only the crispness of night air and broad-leaf trees greeted him.

Duncan crawled out and let the flap down. He felt for the seedling. It was about a pod high. Ah, relief. The clue—it was a conifer amid broadleaf wood plants. Even if one of the roach warriors happened onto this place, they were ignorant when it came to plant species and would not notice the out-of-place conifer. He felt all around, twitched his antennae again, and pressed the place into his memory.

His father's words came back to him. "Once you reach the surface, turn to your right. Go 200 paces and you will reach the far edge of the grove away from the colony. Then you will see the stars."

One, two…thirty, thirty-one…eighty-eight…one hundred forty…. He could see the edge of the grove, but he counted the full 200. A short bush stood at the edge with taller wood plants all around it. He broke one branch backward toward the way he had come. Once in the meadow, he looked at the shape of the dark line of wood plants against the night sky—one seemed taller than the rest and it loomed right above the bush. Yes, he would recognize it.

"Essence, I trust in you to guide my pods," he repeated over and over. He looked up at the stars, which seemed like old friends, even though it had been several season cycles since he had been with his father on the surface at night. He marveled at the accuracy of the chart that his father had made. One star in a group he had memorized seemed to twinkle more brightly indicating the way he was supposed to go.

While aware that more than one predator hunted at night, Duncan felt a strange confidence. He crossed two streams, one small, and one larger but shallow enough not to concern him, in the order he had memorized. He guessed that it was about three h-units past midnight (five h-units since he had left) when his antennae warned him of the edge of the fire ant colony's surface area. He curved to the left, keeping the scent marks well to his right. He had been told that fire ants generally kept to themselves unless a creature entered what they considered their hunting territory. Anything that came onto their surface was fair game. Dairying ants avoided them because they were known to be fierce hunters and fighters and their sting was lethal.

"Essence, I trust in you to guide my pods and protect me," Duncan whispered into the night.

Half a Time Frame
before Duncan's Escape from His Colony

Dagan and Dailey took the lead at dawn at the head of a column of ants leaving their dairying colony. They would march south for half a day and arrive at the harvester colony by midday—if they kept up a good pace. They, and all those behind them, carried baskets filled with jugs of honeydew and grasshopper meat. They had made this trip each full moon for the last several time frames. Their colony's plastic mine had run dry. They had to have plastic for their young. The harvester colony had more than they needed, and they liked the new foods the dairier ants brought to them on such a regular basis.

Dailey shifted her load and glanced behind her. It was the first trip for several carrier trainees and they were lagging behind. "Put your head down and watch the pods of those in front of you. That will balance your load better," she called back to encourage them. The young adults, not yet used to heavy loads over a long distance, continued to lag.

Dagan signaled a halt. "Snack and water break," he declared. The youngsters put their baskets down with a grateful sigh. Dagan turned to his mate and co-leader. "We must be considerate of our trainees," he reminded Dailey. "Remember your first trip?"

She smiled back. "Yes, I was tired, too."

"Besides, if we arrive late, it won't matter much. I'm sure our harvester friends will allow us to spend the night and begin fresh in the morning. Council Chief Dahlia told me last evening that through careful management, we have built up a two-time-frame supply of plastic. She wants to build up a six-time-frame supply in case of emergency."

"Why didn't you tell me earlier?"

"You were asleep when I came home from my meeting with her. I'm sorry; I meant to tell you at breakfast, but I forgot after taking our larva to the nursery. I did remember to tell the nursery workers that we might be gone overnight, though."

Dailey munched half of her dried grasshopper meat snack and drank half of her jug of water. "Good, then we can stop for lunch, too." She rose and went to check on each of the carrying team, checking the youngsters carefully to be sure their appendage joints were not swollen. She was glad to see that all were doing well so far.

"Let's move out," Dagan called out.

The line of ants moved off. They stopped again when the sun was high in the sky and ate the last of their supplies. An h-unit later, they could see the harvester mound ahead of them. A couple of field workers waved front pods back and forth rapidly as they drew closer. Dagan and Daily waved back in a friendly manner.

The field workers ran toward them. "Stop, stop! Go back!" they called in warning.

But it was too late.

Several roach warriors surrounded the line of burdened ants.

"What's going on?" Dagan asked.

"I'm so sorry," one of the field workers said. "We had no way to warn you sooner. These roaches have taken over our colony. We are slaves to them now." He hung his head.

"So we can't trade anymore?" Dailey asked with dismay.

One warrior, who seemed to be in charge, pushed the field workers away from the dairying ants. Then the other roach warriors pointed to the baskets and to the ground. They opened their mandibles and hissed.

Dagan set down his basket, afraid he was about to be injured or worse. The others followed his example. The roaches dragged the baskets away from the ants. Then they hissed again and pointed to the ants, indicating they should leave.

Dailey, Dagan, and their fellow carrying ants backed away slowly. "Perhaps if we leave quietly, we will not be harmed," Dagan said. He could see terror in the eyes of the new, young carriers. He was fairly sure his eyes had the same look. He was having difficulty remaining calm as their leader. Once they had a hundred f-units between themselves and the roaches, Dagan shouted, "Run!"

They ran for nearly half an h-unit at top speed in spite of how tired they all were. Finally, Daily slowed down and stopped. "We must rest," she said.

"What do we do?" the others all asked at once.

"They even kept our baskets!"

"We consumed all our travel supplies!"

"Calm down, everyone," Daily said. "We must rest and think a few minutes." She tried not to show her own worry. Panic would leave them even more vulnerable.

"I didn't drink all my water," one veteran carrier said. "I have a little to share. Also, I sensed a stream only a little way off our trail maybe another half h-unit away."

Dagan took charge. "Yes, I sensed it, too, but I didn't want to stop our trip. We have lost much, but we can travel faster without our burdens. We'll find the stream and drink there. Then we'll set a pace twice as fast and be home before dark."

"But what about plastic for our young? My mate just laid another egg," one carrier said.

"Let's just get ourselves home first," Dagan said. He shared what Council Chief Dahlia had told him the evening before. "Our council has some time to form a new plan."

The group, which had set out with such light hearts, hustled their pods back toward their colony. They found the stream, refreshed themselves and pushed on in spite of rising feelings of despair. An exhausted and dejected group filed into the colony just after darkness fell.

"Go on home to your families," Dailey said. "Please, as you tell the news, try not to sound panicked. Dagan and I will go to our council now and let them know what happened. Our wise leaders will find an answer."

Council Chief Dahlia was shocked to hear their news, but she quickly reassured Dagan and Dailey. "We have a sister dairying colony a day's journey to the north-north-east, and another one farther away to our west. We will have to consult some rather old maps, but we have time to prepare an emissary group to see about trading with them for plastic. There is a fire ant colony in between us and our closest sister colony, but we should be able to go around their surface area."

17.

The Night of Duncan's Escape

Fauna, a fire ant scout, turned to her partner. "What is one dairying ant doing on a journey in the middle of the night?"

"I don't know," Fane replied, "but whoever it is respects our boundaries."

"Go tell Captain Farr. I'll keep an eye out. If I'm not in the same position, I'll be parallel to that ant."

Fane scurried away. It wasn't long before he returned with their captain. Fauna was on the march, her trail well marked for them. When Fane and Captain Farr caught up to her, all three could see the lone dairying ant continuing its path just outside their surface area.

The captain watched for a few minutes, and then said. "Well, that ant is certainly not a threat to us, but there must be some important reason for a night journey. This is highly unusual for that ant variety. In all my training, I've never known dairying ants to travel alone, much less at night."

They paralleled the dairying ant until he (or she—the two fire ant scouts couldn't tell which from that distance) was completely clear of their area.

Then Captain Farr spoke again. "You two, go back the way we came and then follow that ant's trail back to wherever it came from. Turn off your scent markers, stay out of sight, but see what you can find out. Do nothing, except to report back to me."

"Yes, Captain," the pair of scouts replied.

The two expert scouts followed the dairying ant's trail to the northeast. Neither had been through this area before, but that did not matter. Even though they were not leaving a scent trail for their return, their antennae picked up other markers they would be able to follow, and it would be daylight on the way back.

Just before dawn, they found the place in the grove of wood plants from which Duncan had emerged. They looked at the conifer sapling. The male scout reached out. "What in the—"

"No, leave it be," Fauna whispered. "Our captain said to do nothing. Only watch. Let's climb this tall wood plant."

The two climbed nearly to the top and settled in a spot where leaves concealed them but they could see the back slope of the dairying mound and the meadows surrounding it. Dawn broke and the two watched as the colony came to life. Just to their east, they saw several dairying ants around a herd of grasshoppers. As one of them moved away into the meadow, a roach rose up from the grass and pointed him back to his group.

"Roaches?" Fauna exclaimed.

"Hush!" Fane whispered. "Remember, we must not be seen. I hope your voice didn't carry that far. I've been told roaches have excellent hearing."

The two huddled closer to the trunk of the wood plant. No heads or antennae turned in their direction. They continued to watch as a large group of ants, guiding perhaps fifty aphids and with several roaches around them, emerged from what they guessed was the colony's main entrance—the entrance itself was on the opposite side of the mound, which they could not see directly. The ants guided the aphids into a grove of smaller wood plants perhaps 200 f-units to the west of the mound. The aphids scampered into the wood plants and settled themselves to suck the plants' sap. Some ants climbed after them—seemingly to tend them—while others remained at the base of the plants.

"I wish we knew how to get our food like that. Hunting has become so difficult the last few season cycles," Fauna said, remembering to whisper this time.

Fane nodded. "But why do those roaches seem to guard them?"

"I don't know. I've never read about any ants inviting roaches to live with them. Have you?"

Fane shook his head. "But I do remember reading in our colony Antstory book about how roaches tried to invade our colony once. It was a great victory for us. They've never come close again, except for a few, from time to time, who seem to be watching what we are doing."

Fauna smiled. "Yes, I remember that lesson, too. You don't suppose…. They don't have our natural defenses…."

Fane shrugged his thorax up and down. "I think it's time to leave and report what we've seen."

"Yes, but we'd better stay low and move slowly until we are at least a d-unit away, and keep our antennae up in case any roaches are close by."

The two doubled their pace once they were well on the way back to their colony. They stopped briefly to drink water and eat a bit of dried beetle meat they carried in their satchels. Both had been on duty now for way over twelve h-units, and they were tired, but they did not slow their pace.

Captain Farr met them at the edge of the colony's surface area. He looked tired, too. "I was beginning to worry. What did you find?"

Fauna related the story. "The ant's track led us to a spot of disturbed earth with a tiny conifer plant—way out of place in a grove of broad-leafed wood plants. I thought it must mark something, but we did not touch it. We climbed a wood plant and watched for an h-unit. Captain, there were roaches that seemed to be in charge of the dairying ants. It was very strange to us!"

"Roaches? In my mother's young adult days, she fought them away from our colony."

"We thought of that, too, from basic Antstory," Fauna continued. "We were too far away to see much more, so we came back."

"You two go on to your domiciles and get a good day's sleep. I'll take this news to Council Chief Fredrika."

Dawn was breaking as Duncan reached his goal after an almost ten h-unit journey. He had stopped briefly two times to drink water and eat some dried grasshopper meat he had carried with him, but he had consumed the last of his supplies three h-units ago. Although his appendages ached after an entire night's journey, his heart surged with excitement that he had arrived at his destination without getting lost. The dairying colony mound loomed not far in the distance, and Duncan could see a group of herders tending to grasshoppers less than a quarter d-unit away.

He called out to them. "My fellow dairying ants, please help me! I have traveled a long way and must see your council chief on behalf of my colony."

One ant left the group immediately and ran to him. "My name is Dara. How may I help you?"

Duncan gasped, suddenly feeling more exhausted than he ever had in his life. "My colony, a sister colony to yours, has been enslaved by roaches. They refuse us plastic for our young, who are dying. We need help to get the roaches out of our colony. Please, I must talk to your council chief." Then his legs gave out and he collapsed in a heap.

Duncan was vaguely aware as Dara picked him up and began to carry him. The next thing he knew, he was lying on a cushion inside a colony chamber. Three ants looked down on him. He jerked, flinging his legs outward.

"Do not fear. You are safe now. I am Dahlia, this colony's council chief. Dara, here," she gestured to the young female who had first greeted Duncan in the meadow, "told me what you said about your colony. And this is Dagny, our spiritual guide. Drink some honeydew and then tell me all."

Duncan took the mug held out to him and emptied it into his mouth. "Thank you. How long have I been asleep?"

"Most of the morning," Dahlia answered. "We thought it wise to let you rest before asking you more about what has happened to our sister colony."

"It started about twenty season cycles ago," Duncan began. As he continued the tale, Dahlia handed him food and honey dew. Between bites and drinks, he explained that for many season cycles before he hatched, the roaches had treated their ant slaves well enough, but now things had grown much worse. He related the dreams of Master Daeira that had been taught to him and many other details. Finally he said,

"And so, I was chosen, because I also had dreams, to escape and seek help from you."

Dagny reached out and stroked Duncan gently. "Essence has surely guided your journey to us. I had a dream last night, too, very similar to the one you described from you and your spiritual guide, about the unification of ants. And I saw you in my dream, coming to us."

"Thank Essence!" Duncan said. "You will help us, then?"

"Yes, we will try, but many problems have to be solved as to how. Let me gather the council together so we may discuss everything. Please, let Dara show you where the sanitation area in her domicile is so you may refresh your body." Dahlia turned to Dara. "Will you continue to take care of him while Dagny and I summon the council? Then please guide him to the Council Chamber."

"Yes, of course. Duncan, are you rested enough to stand now?"

"Yes, I think so. I'm sorry to be a burden to you. You brought me to your own home? Thank you."

"You were no burden. I was working with my parents when we saw you. They told me to bring you here. Let me show you where you may bathe."

First Day of Duncan's Absence from His Colony

Rashad was frustrated. Everywhere he had looked for the messenger, Duncan, the one spending so much time with Master Daeira, he had been unable to locate him. His first stop had been around midday at the entrance of the plastic mine.

"You missed him," the mine entrance ant said. "He has already been here. Sorry."

"Do you know where he was headed?"

"I'm sorry, Rashad. I have no idea. Sometimes he comes here in the morning; other times he comes in the afternoon. You might check at the message center. Maybe they can tell you his route."

Rashad didn't bother to say thank you. He headed for the message center. Upon reaching there, he asked the coordinator, "Where might I find Duncan at this time of the day?"

"Hum, let me see if I can find his route," the coordinator said.

Rashad tapped one back pod impatiently. The coordinator shuffled several pieces of parchment around for quite some time before saying, "Here's his usual route; you may look it over, but please don't take it. This is my only copy."

Rashad took a piece of parchment from his own satchel and asked for an ink pot. He jotted down all the locations after midday, handed back the ink pot and stomped out.

When Rashad arrived at the next possible colony location and asked for Duncan, again he heard, "He's already been here; sorry."

He skipped Duncan's next usual place and went on to the one after that, where he heard, "I'm sorry, Rashad; I haven't seen him yet today. But sometimes if he doesn't have a message for us, he doesn't stop by. We didn't have any messages for him to pick up, so I didn't put out our 'pick up' notice."

So it went all along the route. Rashad thought about going to Duncan's domicile, but why do that? Both his parents would be out working at their job sites, and Duncan was out somewhere—likely going up one tunnel as Rashad went down a different one—just missing each other. He stormed into Master Daeira's domicile. Those two are up to something! he thought.

He found Master Daeira alone, sitting on her usual floor cushion, deep in meditation. From past experience, he knew he could do nothing but wait for her to acknowledge his presence. He wondered why he continued to let her do this.

"Where is Duncan?" he demanded when she finally opened her eyes to glare at him. He ignored her insolence as he always did. He understood her feelings toward him better than she probably thought he did. He also knew she would never understand how he was stuck in the middle, so there was no point in trying to discuss it with her.

Master Daeira looked deeply into Rashad's eyes—how he hated it when she did that. It was as though she could see inside him. "Why do you need him?" the spiritual guide asked in an irritatingly calm voice.

"I need to talk to him about keeping to his schedule so if I need to find him, I can."

"Oh, is that all? He always stops by here at some time during the day—you know I'm training him to be an assistant spiritual guide—but he has not arrived yet today. The last time I saw him, I did notice that he seemed awfully tired. I told him he should see someone at the medical facility for a checkup. Maybe he's there. If he comes by after you leave, I'll tell him to go to your domicile. Will that be all right?"

Rashad left. It was long past the end of his workday. He was tired and hungry, but he headed for the medical center anyway. It had closed for the day when he got there. He pounded his back pods on the ground in anger.

The roach warrior on duty at the nearby cross tunnel approached. "Rashad, something wrong?"

Rashad stomped once more to get it out of his system. "Yes. I don't suppose you saw that messenger ant named Duncan come here today, did you?"

"At least thirty ants went in the clinic today, not to mention the ones who passed through these two tunnels. They all look the same to me. I don't know any of their names. Don't really want to."

"Never mind," Rashad said. He thought again about going to Duncan's domicile—surely he would be home by now—but he was too tired and hungry to care. He gave up for the day.

The following morning, he left his domicile early and went directly to the message center, hoping to catch Duncan before he left there. Several messengers ran by him, but not Duncan. Was it his imagination, or were they in a greater hurry than usual?

The portal to the message center was already open when he got there—early even for that facility.

"Good morning, Rashad," the coordinator said, much too cheerfully for Rashad's taste. "If you are still looking for Duncan, I'm afraid you've missed him again. I didn't see him come in, but his pile of messages is already gone, so he must have been here. In fact, every messenger has already picked up their satchel. I was planning to tell Duncan that you were looking for him, but I missed him, too."

"You will let me have that 'one' copy of his route."

"Yes, of course, but I must tell you that sometimes the messengers trade routes with each other so they know every route—in case of emergency." He handed the parchment to Rashad.

Rashad chased along the route half the morning—getting lost twice in new tunnels he was not familiar with because his many duties kept him from checking on every little thing—before he caught up with, not Duncan, but a female messenger.

"Why are you on Duncan's route? Where is Duncan?" he shouted.

The young female stared at him, shaking.

"What's the matter? Have you no voice?"

She stammered, "Um...I'm sorry. Um...I'm new. Part of my training is to, is to...trade routes, and this, this...was my day to trade with Duncan."

Rashad forced himself not to yell. "And what is your usual route?"

"I...don't have a regular route yet." The young female slumped to the ground. "I'm sorry. I'm sorry." She burst into sobs. "Please, mercy, mercy."

Rashad suppressed a scream. He waved her on with his front pod. "Go! Get on your way."

Many other issues around the colony needed his attention. He didn't have more time to waste chasing Duncan. But as he went about his other business he told everyone, ant and roach alike, in their respective languages, "Tell the messenger Duncan I need to see him as soon as possible! No excuses!"

At this point, he hated the ants; he hated his employer; he hated what his life had become. Worst of all, he hated to admit even to himself that he admired many things about the ants he so hated at that moment.

Third Day of Duncan's Absence

The message coordinator was the one to take Master Daeira her messages at the end of that day. "Is there any news? How long do you expect Duncan to be gone? I don't know how much longer we can keep this up. I think Rashad suspects something."

"He should have reached our sister colony yesterday morning," Daeira replied. "He knows he must return as quickly as possible. All we can do now is to lift up our thoughts to Essence."

The coordinator nodded. "Rashad frightened one of the new messengers to tears. Remember when the council decided to close the pottery-making facility? About the same time, two of our oldest messengers had to retire for health reasons. So we got this female—about the same age as Duncan, I'd say, because there aren't any younger ones—from there and have been retraining her. I should have given his stack someone more experienced. I will tomorrow."

"Ah, I just thought of this! Perhaps you could tell all the messengers there is a little game to see who can deliver all of someone else's messages the most quickly."

"Great idea. But what if—"

Master Daeira took the coordinator's front pods in hers and held them briefly. "Let Essence and me worry about that."

18.

First Day of Duncan's Stay at the Sister Dairying Colony

After Duncan had bathed, Dara led him through her colony's tunnels to the Council Chamber. Duncan felt a bit overwhelmed by the size of the chamber and the number of ants seated on cushions around a large, oval table. This colony must have a population at least three times that of mine, he thought.

"Ah, Duncan, welcome again. Please, come and sit here beside me. Dara, do you wish to stay with us?"

"I wish I could, but I should get back to the surface and tell my parents and the others what is happening."

"Ah, yes, of course."

Duncan settled his abdomen on the cushion between Dahlia and Dagny. She introduced all the council members and then said, "Please, do not worry about remembering all our names. Will you repeat your story for us?"

Duncan nodded and then, with a few more details, recounted the highlights of what had happened to his colony: how Rashad first arrived; how Master Daeira had taught Rashad to speak Ant; about Sir Rainart's relatively benevolent control; how Master Daeira had foreseen a possible lack of plastic and how everyone in every family had hidden plastic in their homes.

He recounted how the hidden plastic had run out long before his own emergence into adulthood; how they had tried to fight back; about their despair and that there had been no mating ceremonies since the fourth season cycle of his larvahood. He related the consequences of declining population and increased work, closing the training facilities, and the difficulties of parents trying to teach the last intelligent young adults in their homes after working all day, as well as caring for those who emerged from pupation plastic-deprived.

"Then I began to have dreams," he continued. "Master Daeira started teaching me more about deep meditation after my own workday ended. I had a dream of coming to you to ask for help. So here I am. Thank you for your kindness. I hope you will be able to help us."

Duncan looked at the group and noticed each ant's reaction to his story. Some grumbled in anger and shook their heads as they repeated "Roaches" over and over; others looked as if they were about to weep; a few hung their heads. No one spoke.

Dagny broke the silence. "To all of you here, I have also had dreams of what Duncan says." She reached out and stroked the back of Duncan's thorax. "At first, I almost didn't believe my dreams could be real. When I first heard this from Duncan in Dara's home, my heart ached from the pain of so many young suffering and dying from lack of plastic. But in the h-unit since, Essence spoke quietly to me that while this may be the grievous event, it was what would be needed to bring about something much greater—that we might never have done unless spurred on by tragedy—the unification of many colonies into something much better for all ants. I know Essence will reveal much more in the next few days and time frames."

"How?" "What do you mean?" "What now for us?" were among the murmurs throughout the chamber.

Dahlia raised one front pod. The chamber fell silent. "I have not had a chance to tell Duncan of our own problems," she began. "You see, Duncan, your arrival is at an unfortunate time for us. Our plastic mine ran dry early last season cycle. We had been trading our food products for plastic with a colony of harvester ants about half-a-day's journey to the south. Our last trade trip was less than half a time frame ago and our trade group returned empty-podded. Roaches have taken over that colony as well! We were going to send a delegation tomorrow to request plastic from you, our sister colony."

Duncan's head dropped forward.

"But, everyone, please listen," Dahlia continued. "As Dagny said, this is also a time of great hope. Remember that we decided to establish an emergency supply of plastic. We have enough for two time frames—more if all adults stop consuming it, as Duncan said his colony did. We have other sister colonies, a bit more distant, but reachable. We will make plans immediately to send delegations to them to ask them to supply us with plastic. And to help Duncan's colony, as well. I trust in Essence to show us the way."

An idea popped into Duncan's head along with part of his dream and he blurted out, "I passed a fire ant colony on my way here. Why not ask them to help, too?"

His comment was met with startled silence, but Duncan pressed the point. "My dream wasn't just about dairying ants, but all kinds of ants. We either ask for their help, or perish one colony at a time." He remained standing, his front pods reaching out to them, begging for their support.

The assistant council chief spoke up. "That would be a very dangerous thing to do. Remember the group of our herders who accidentally strayed onto their surface? All the hoppers—and our members, too—were killed, and presumably eaten. That was only one generation ago."

Others nodded. Dahlia explained to Duncan that all young adults were taught exactly how far to go on the surface in the direction of the fire ant colony and no farther.

Dagny's voice rose above the din. "Yes, it may be dangerous. But Duncan is right. I saw fire ants in my dream, too, and they were with us, not against us."

Dahlia rose from her cushion. "I propose that we send out several delegations. I will go to the fire ants with you, Duncan. Dagny, will you join us?"

Mandibles of several council members opened wide in shock.

"Yes," Dagny replied. She rose and took one of Duncan's pods in hers. Dahlia did the same with Duncan's other front pod.

One by one, the council members rose and reached out to those on either side, joining their pods to those already standing. The assistant council chief finally stood and joined them, completing the oval.

"May we leave as soon as possible?" Duncan asked. "My fellow messengers are covering for my absence, but if I am gone too long, Rashad, the roach interpreter, will notice and it will go badly for everyone."

"We will leave at dawn tomorrow morning," Dahlia replied. "Dagny, we have many other plans to make. Would you mind taking Duncan to your domicile where he may rest again to be ready for our journey? I'll come for both of you an h-unit before daybreak and tell you what else we decide here."

"Of course." She reached out one front pod for Duncan. "Please, join me. I'd like to hear more about your dreams and those of Master Daeira."

Duncan followed his guide through several tunnels and levels. Although he was a stranger, he felt welcomed by the familiar odor of the tunnels. Dagny's comfortable quarters were much like Master Daeira's and his own.

She pointed to a soft cushion and said, "Please, make yourself at home. I'm going to put some roast grasshopper left from yesterday in the heating box."

Dagny handed Duncan a mug of honeydew. He wanted to gulp it down quickly but restrained himself in an effort to be polite. He didn't remember later what time they stopped eating and talking.

The next thing Duncan knew, Dagny was tapping his thorax. "Duncan, wake up. Dahlia is here. It's time to go."

He followed the two females through several tunnels until they reached the surface. "Will I see Dara again?" he asked.

Dahlia smiled at him. "It's quite likely. We'll pass one of the herds on our way."

When they reached the surface, they were joined by two carriers bearing heavily loaded baskets full of dried grasshopper meat and some of the seeds from the harvester colony.

"We will carry them from here," Dahlia said. "I am hoping the gifts and only three of us will convey our peaceful intentions."

Duncan crawled beneath one of the baskets before the carrier set it down, but he could not hold it long. "I'm sorry. My parents once said that when they were young, all colony members learned to do many jobs, but the roaches closed the training centers. I thought I could do it, but I've never been taught how to handle these."

"There is no need for you to apologize. Your offer was sincere," Dagny reassured him. "Dahlia and I had planned to do this anyway."

The trio passed Dara and her parents as they and others were moving the grasshopper herd to another grazing area. Dara took both Duncan's front pods in hers. Her touch stirred something in him that he had never felt before, followed by a sudden feeling of shyness. Words failed him.

"We will have all of you in our thoughts to Essence," Dara said, "and, Duncan, I hope we will see each other again one day. I'd like to be able to get to know you better."

"I'd...I'd...like that, too."

The sun began its long climb up the sky. Neither Dahlia nor Dagny spoke. It took great concentration to carry the loaded baskets. Duncan found himself in the lead, warning the others of rough places so they did not stumble. All of them knew, if they simply headed northeast, they would reach the fire ant surface territory by midday.

Duncan's mind wandered about in odd directions. What if the fire ants attack? If they don't attack, what if they refuse to help us? What will happen to my colony, my family? But I know we must succeed... my dreams...Dara...but if Master Daeira wants me to continue to train with her...become a spiritual guide...which means not having a mate and family...or maybe not...Dara.... Must all spiritual guides never have families? I don't remember learning anything like that... but maybe my parents didn't have time.... Dara was so kind, and the way she touched me in a simple greeting.... Master Daeira said it was her personal choice.... She never said she had to remain single.... Oh, get this out of my head. I've got to stay focused on the moment and the day....

On and on his brain went in circles with Dara popping into it constantly. He had never spent any time with the females his age in his own colony. There didn't seem to be much point in it since no one could, or would, mate under the circumstances, and he had never had the time or energy to do anything but work, and meditate with

Master Daeira, and sleep. He had felt called to this task and answered that call. But now…there was the real possibility of freedom, home, and maybe even a family of his own…. He found himself hoping, wanting, to spend a lot of time with Dara.

The scent markers at the edge of the fire ant colony's surface brought Duncan back from the faraway place his mind had taken him. He stopped.

"We should go on a little farther," Dagny said, "and then stop. That might let them know we wish to communicate while respecting their borders."

The three went on perhaps 200 f-units and then the two females eased themselves from beneath the baskets and sat down to rest. Not even a moment passed before half-a-dozen fire ants rose from the meadow grass around them. Duncan gave a startled cry. None of them had sensed the presence of any living creature nearby.

One of the fire ants stepped forward. "I am Captain Farr. Two of my scouts, Fane and Fauna, watched your journey," he pointed to Duncan, "the night before last. Something didn't seem quite right. We have been on the lookout for you and mean you no harm."

Duncan jumped when the fire ant pointed to him. The dairying ants might have been larger, but the fire ant's huge mandibles and pointed abdomen—from which the tip of his stinger could be seen—still frightened him. His sigh of relief at the words "mean you no harm" was audible.

"I am Dahlia, Council Chief of the Dairying Colony almost five h-units journey away. Our intentions are peaceful," Dahlia said. "We wish to speak to your council chief to discuss difficulties we are having and how we hope you might be able to help us, and how we might help you in return."

"Please, follow me," Captain Farr said. Two fire ants easily picked up the baskets and the group walked on toward the colony.

In less than half an h-unit, Dagny, Dahlia, and Duncan sat comfortably in shallow hollows filled with dry leaves on the fire ant's Council Chamber's floor, arranged in an oval like that in the dairying colonies. The two fire ants who had carried the baskets set them down in the center of the oval. Then they brought mugs of water to the three dairying ants and dishes of cooked wild beetle meat. Captain Farr stayed with them while they waited for the council to assemble.

Several fire ants entered, settling into the hollows until all the hollows were filled. One female fire ant, who was larger than the others, spoke. "I am Fredrika, Council Chief. We welcome you as our guests. I would also like to put to rest something long past—an unfortunate incident during my parents' time. It seems some ants of your colony lost their way and wandered onto our surface. Two scouts found their remains; a mantis attacked them by the look of it, we were told. It is our custom to cover the remains of a creature where it fell and place a small marker there later. Captain Farr will be glad to show you the place. The council back then decided not to approach your colony, thinking your members might fear we were attacking."

Dahlia nodded her thanks, and thought, That's a relief! Back then, we probably would have thought they intended us harm.

Fredrika gestured to Duncan. "Please, tell us why you have come."

So, to this new and still slightly fear-inspiring audience, Duncan related what had happened to his colony.

When he finished, Captain Farr lifted one front pod to speak. Fredrika nodded to him.

"Pardon my forwardness, Duncan. I didn't mean to startle you when I pointed to you on the surface," the captain said. "When Fauna and Fane saw you the other night, they thought it was very unusual for a dairying ant to be traveling at night, and alone. We all saw how you respected our borders. Later, I had Fauna and Fane follow your trail back. While keeping out of sight in the tall wood plant near the place from which you came out of the escape tunnel you described, they observed roaches outside your colony. They were on the back side of your colony where they could not see clearly and were under strict orders from me not to be seen or interfere. Your story confirms what we suspected, but such cruelty...." He shook his head and antennae.

Fredrika gestured toward Dahlia, who then described at length her colony's urgent need for plastic, their trade relationship with the harvester colony, and its fall to roach control.

Fredrika rose from her seated position. Everyone looked toward the colony's leader.

She began with a gesture toward a very old female fire ant who had been introduced as the colony's spiritual guide, but who had not said anything as yet. "This certainly explains your strange dreams of late, doesn't it, Faith?"

The old female nodded.

Fredrika continued. "The time has indeed come for all ants to unite. Here in my colony, we protect even our weakest members. Why shouldn't we extend that to other kinds of ants? Our ways of hunting are not sufficient anymore. You may be hungry for plastic, but we are often hungry for food of any kind! If you will share your food with us, and teach us how to grow food and manage herds as you do, so that we may have a better life, we will give you our protection. We should not let the roaches enslave any of us. The roaches know better than to attack us, but they watch constantly. They will see if a force of us sets out to free your colony. Commander Fadi, what would you suggest?"

During the council chief's speech, all the council members had been nodding their heads in agreement. Duncan wanted to cry out in joy—his colony would be saved—but he kept quiet, waiting like the others to hear what Guard Commander Fadi would propose.

Fadi rose. "The attack plan seems obvious to me. If Duncan escaped through a tunnel, then we can attack through one! Those roaches would be completely unprepared for an underground attack of the size I have in mind. Plus, we would need to tunnel to this harvester colony, too. They can't be left to the fate Duncan's colony has suffered. This is not something that can be done in a day or two, because these tunnels must be large enough for four guards to march thorax to thorax. We'll need help from our sister colonies, and from yours," he gestured to Dahlia, "for supplies and extra workers. Tunneling is not my area of expertise, but I will ready all our fighting guards for the battle to come."

Duncan could hardly believe what he was hearing. Hope surged through him. The feeling was contagious. A babble of voices rose in the chamber.

Fredrika raised a pod for silence. "Clearly, we have much planning to do, but not all at once. Duncan, I sensed from your story that you must return to your colony soon."

Duncan nodded.

"I want you to trust that we will plan this and carry it out. You must rest for a few h-units. As soon as it is dark, Fauna and Fane will escort you safely back to your escape tunnel. They will relate more of our plans along the way. Captain Farr, will you please take this brave young male to guest quarters and inform Fauna and Fane of their new task?"

Captain Farr rose and reached out his pod to Duncan. Before Duncan followed the captain, he embraced Dagny and Dahlia. He repeated, "Thank you, thank you," over and over to everyone.

19.

Two Days after Duncan's Escape,
Second Time Frame, 1 B.C.C.

Rest was impossible for Duncan that afternoon. He was far too excited even to think about it. Captain Farr sensed as much. As they reclined in hollows like those in the Council Chamber, Captain Farr struck up a lively conversation, asking more about Duncan and his colony.

Duncan answered all of Captain Farr's questions and then asked, "Why didn't we sense your presence when we came? We could smell your border markings so clearly."

Captain Farr smiled and then explained, "We can turn our scent-producing organs on and off. If we couldn't, we would never catch any food at all. The training of those of us who guard or hunt is not considered complete until we can 'shadow' our trainer, staying within striking distance without our trainer knowing it—and my trainer had better antennae than either you or I do, better hearing, too," he laughed. "There was one time I was sure I had passed the test until my trainer said, 'You've gotten better, Farr, but you aren't good enough yet. I heard a twig snap.' He pointed to exactly where I was hidden." The captain laughed at the memory, but Duncan was serious.

"You could take over any colony you wanted, couldn't you?"

"Theoretically, yes, but that is not our way. Ancient stories we are taught state that there was a time when our species was aggressive, even sometimes killing without reason, but that was many eons ago in our evolution. Essence has guided us to keep to ourselves, hunting for what we need, staying within our hunting areas, protecting our own by challenging any who cross our warning scents, but leaving alone those who respect us, as we did when you carefully went around."

"I wish we had known that long ago," Duncan said.

"I wish so, too. But we can't change the past, only the future. Would you mind waiting here? I really should get back to the Council Chamber. I'll need to brief Fauna and Fane before they take you home. You'll find things to amuse yourself in that cupboard," he said as he pointed to a small wooden door about halfway up the chamber wall. "Someone will bring you food again in the evening."

Duncan investigated the contents of the cupboard as soon as Captain Farr left. He found a board with some sort of map—he presumed of the colony area—and a bunch of miniature carved fire ants in two different colors. He thought it must be a game, but he had no one to play it with, and no idea of the rules. Next to it were several bound manuscripts. He picked up one and settled down to read. He was several pages into some of the colony's history when two fire ants entered the chamber.

"I am Fauna and this is Fane," the female said. "We have brought you the evening meal. As soon as we have all eaten, we will leave."

Duncan rose from the hollow and reached out his pods in greeting. Fane set down the food on a flat surface nearby. Both fire ants offered their front pods in return.

Fauna spoke as Duncan drank broth from a large mug. "Captain Farr told us that the council is still deep in planning, but we know we must take you back tonight. For now, tell your colony members they will be free before this season cycle ends. In order to be an effective surprise, our attack on the roaches in your colony and in the harvester colony must begin on the same day and at the same time. If one attack happens sooner, the roaches would have a chance to warn the other group. It will take several time frames to complete tunnels from here to your colony, between ours and the other dairying colony, and from the dairying colony to the harvester colony. We can't risk having roach spies catch any hint of what is going on beneath their pods. We do see them spy on us from time to time."

Fauna stopped to drink her broth while Fane continued. "Delegations will go out from our colony to our sister fire ant colonies and from the dairying colony to their sister colony, and on to others we may not yet know about. We will be requesting workers to help build the tunnels as quickly as possible and to provide extra food. We will be supplying Dahlia's colony with the plastic they need, and they will feed us. That way, workers who hunted before can help dig the tunnels. The two dairying ants who led the last trade trip will go to the harvester colony to let those ants know that we plan to free them. A couple of our guards will go with them to make sure they are safe."

Fauna set down her mug and resumed the instructions they had been told. "When we get you back to your escape tunnel, we must make a little place at the entrance where we can leave news each time frame and where you can tell us what is happening with you. The first thing we will need is a map of your colony so we can find the best spot from which to break forth in attack. We will need to know how many roaches will oppose us and if that number changes. We will leave notes the night of the new moon each time frame with news and any questions we have."

Duncan had finished his meal. "Thank you. That soup was delicious. Will it matter who picks up the messages and answers your questions each time frame?"

"Probably not, but we thought it would be you. Why?" Fauna replied.

"I have a feeling I'll be carefully watched once I return."

Another guard entered the chamber. "It's completely dark. Time to leave."

Duncan and the two fire ants remained silent as a precaution on the journey back to his colony, but the trip was uneventful. When they reached the flap of sod that covered the escape tunnel entrance, Duncan lifted it carefully. He quickly scooped out a small ledge about half the length of his pod down, and then pointed to it and gestured writing. His two escorts nodded. Fane pointed up at the tiny crescent, made the motions for a waxing and waning moon, and pointed to the ledge again. Duncan nodded and crawled down the narrow tunnel, welcoming the total darkness that engulfed him as one of the fire ants replaced the sod flap.

When Duncan emerged from the tunnel into the pottery storage room, he felt a pod grab him. "I'm so glad to see you, but be silent," whispered the one who had guided him when he escaped.

They waited in silence behind a stack of bowls used to serve food. Duncan could hear roach voices outside the storage chamber. The two barely breathed. When the voices faded, the tunneling ant whispered again. "Have you brought good news? Only yes, or no. Details later."

"Yes," Duncan whispered back.

"Drink this. It's going to make you dizzy, but don't worry. Slip on your messenger satchel. Do not say a word. Let me do everything."

Duncan slipped his front pods through the familiar straps of his message bag, took the mug handed to him, and emptied it into his mouth. The effect was immediate. Duncan slumped to the floor.

He tried to gain control of his muscles as his tunnel-building guide picked him up. His muscles would not obey and the chamber seemed to spin. By the time they left the pottery chamber, he could not even hold his head up.

After a couple of turns in smaller tunnels, the ant carrying Duncan began to shout, even though it was still a few h-units before the earliest of anyone's workday would begin, "Tell everyone! I've found Duncan! I must take him to the medical center. He must have collapsed from exhaustion. Pass the word to his parents that they may know he is safe."

The tunnel-building ant carried Duncan in his front pods, and he whispered to Duncan between his shouts of gladness at having found him. "Don't worry; you'll be fine in a couple of days. Rashad has had all the warriors searching for you. Master Daeira came up with this idea and told me to have you drink that potion the moment you showed up, so we all continue to tell the truth when Rashad asks questions."

Duncan tried to nod, but lost consciousness.

When he awoke, he was surrounded by his parents, Master Daeira, Council Chief Delana, a medical attendant, and Rashad. All of them, except Rashad, were smiling.

Duncan tried to clear his mind. His head throbbed with pain.

But Rashad demanded, "Where have you been?"

Duncan found he couldn't open his mandibles to speak.

Master Daeira spoke for him, "He's been doing his job, Rashad. What else would he be doing? You heard what the tunnel digger who found him said. You saw that one undelivered message from two days ago in his satchel. Its address was very close to where he was found. He must have become disoriented and gone the wrong way to the end of that tunnel where no one could see him."

"All the tunnels were searched this afternoon and patrolled after dark!" Rashad protested. He pointed at Duncan again. "Where have you been?"

Duncan tried again to speak, but what came out was mumbling and gibberish.

"Rashad," Duncan's medical attendant said, "I must protest this harsh questioning. Can't you see how ill from exhaustion he is? Why, he can't even speak right now! I must insist that he remain here at least until tomorrow and then have another day or two of rest at home."

Rashad ground his mandibles at the group and stomped out.

Master Daeira gave Duncan a sign to remain silent, not difficult since he couldn't seem to speak anyway. Duncan's mother began to caress him in joy. The others followed in turn.

"He's left the corridor," Duncan's father said before he embraced his son.

"Can you nod your head?" Master Daeira asked.

Duncan nodded.

"I'm sorry we had to give you such a strong potion. It was the only way we could think of to keep you, and all of us, safe," Master Daeira said.

"I know your head hurts," the medical attendant added, "but that will end in about an h-unit. You'll be fine by tomorrow morning."

Delana explained how they had covered for his absence and Rashad's suspicions.

"I'm going to ask you simple questions for now," Master Daeira said, "We will get the details later. Was your trip successful?"

Duncan nodded.

"Will we receive help?"

Duncan nodded again. He was bursting inside to be able to tell them how wonderful the news was, but that relief would not be immediate.

"Send the good news out through the secret system and say there will be more news in a few days," Delana said to Duncan's father.

Dart caressed his son once more. "I'm so proud of you," he said before he left the chamber.

By the following morning, Duncan was back at home. He told his parents the amazing details of his trip.

"I understand the delay," his mother said, "but waiting longer seems hard to bear after all this time."

"I know it will be hard to wait, but we'll receive news every time frame," Duncan reassured her. "You must also let everyone know that if we seem too excited, the roaches might suspect something."

"You are absolutely right," Dart added. "Rashad really gave us problems while you were away."

They were interrupted by loud thumps on their portal. Rashad barged in the moment Dodie cracked it opened.

Rashad stormed across the chamber to where Duncan reclined on the floor. "Feeling better?" he asked with an unmistakable tone of scorn and sarcasm.

"Yes, thank you," Duncan said, managing to remain calm.

"From now on, you are to report to me every day, exactly at noon, at the entrance to the plastic mine! Is that clear?"

"Yes, I will do that."

"See that you do!" Rashad left as abruptly as he had come.

The details of their coming rescue went out to the entire colony, along with a caution to everyone not to seem too happy when any roaches were near.

Master Daeira came to see Duncan later that evening. After embracing him again, she said, "Your part in this is over for now. Three others will take turns picking up the news at each new moon. We are preparing a very detailed map of the colony. You'll hear the news like everyone else so Rashad will not suspect. I think we will have to suspend your spiritual training for a while, too."

"About that…." Duncan hesitated.

Master Daeira looked at him fondly. "What's troubling you? You may tell me anything."

Duncan sighed, but he knew he had to get this off his mind. "Does everyone who has dreams become a spiritual guide?"

"No, not always."

"Must spiritual guides always remain single?"

Daeira gave him a long, gentle look. "I think I understand where this is going. Duncan, if you do not feel truly called to being a spiritual guide, you shouldn't become one. And you don't have to make up your mind any time soon. I'm sorry if you felt pressured."

"No, it's not that…it's just…well, I think I might want a mate and family."

She smiled. "You should think carefully about either choice. Meditate on it. If you are meant to be a spiritual guide, you will feel it. If not, you will know that, too, and you will meet the right female in good time. Early colony records show that some spiritual guides were mated, but most chose not to."

She gave him a motherly caress before leaving.

20.

End of Second Time Frame, 1 B.C.C.

Dagan and Dailey waited about a quarter d-unit from the colony's main entrance for the two fire ant guards who were to accompany them on their mission to make contact with the harvester colony. The sky was light, but the sun had not yet broken the horizon. Dailey checked the provisions in their satchels—three days of water and food was what they had been told to pack. Everything was there. They had also been told they probably wouldn't see their escorts' approach, so they should try not to be startled and remain as quiet as possible.

A wave of the meadow grass, which could just as easily have been the wind, was the only indication of something approaching before the two fire ants rose only ten f-units away. Dailey nearly jumped out of her exoskeleton but did not cry out.

"Please, drop down into the grass as we are," the guard whispered.

Both dairying ants did as they were told. "I am Fane and this is Fauna," the guard behind Dailey said. "I'm sorry I startled you. We sensed some roaches—they wander around this area from time to time—a few d-units back. We didn't want them to see us approach your colony."

Dailey and Dagan introduced themselves, and then Dagan asked, "Will we have to hide like this the entire journey?"

"It will be safer if we do," Fauna replied.

"That explains why we had to pack provisions for three days. It will be slower traveling that way," Daily said.

"Actually, we should only be gone for two, but it's always best to plan for an extra day, and it's not really that much slower," Fauna said.

Hushed tones continued. "Do you think it's possible that the roaches you sensed would be scouting about to take over our colony?" Dagan asked.

Fain assured them, "We've discussed this with your council chief, but it's not likely. Since your trade trip was sent back, they've probably figured out that you have no plastic. For that reason, they are not likely to bother you. Our commander has appointed more scouts day and night, though, to keep a watch out for any group large enough to mount an attack. A group of roaches that size would be pretty hard to miss! We would be ready for them on your behalf."

"At any rate," Fauna continued, "we've been advised to travel off-trail and leave no scent."

"How will we know where we are, or which way to head, if we can't see anything but tall meadow grass around us?" Dailey wondered.

"We will stay fairly close to the trail you've established for trade," Fauna assured her, "but we will remain unseen. You two will automatically leave small traces of scent, which will guide our return trip. If the roaches sense you, they will just think it's from all the trade trips before. I'll take the lead, you two in the middle, and Fane will come last. Slightly west of south, a bit over thirty-five d-units, correct?"

"Yes," the two dairying ants said together.

The four ants headed out in silence. They took one brief rest about halfway along. It was mid-day when they could see the harvester mound in the distance. Fane signaled a halt. "I'm going to scout around to see where their surface workers are," he whispered, "and where we might be able to speak with them without being seen. Stay here until I return; eat and drink a little. It might be a long day."

Fauna put a front pod to her mandibles, signaling continued silence before she drew her supplies from her satchel. Even as she ate and drank, her antennae swayed above her with the grass—mostly brown and dry as usual for this time of the season cycle—testing the air for the scent of any living thing. She could see in Dailey's eyes the desire to talk, but signaled again to remain silent. Getting to know these new friends would have to wait.

Fauna reviewed the events of the last quarter time frame in her mind. How her job of watching their border had changed since seeing Duncan! She had been used to sleeping by day and patrolling at night.

Now she never knew when she would get a chance to sleep deeply. She and Fane would be making a night trip every time frame to Duncan's colony, and a day trip to this one, too, once they were able to establish regular communication.

The fire ants' world had suddenly expanded way beyond their own territory. In order not to arouse suspicion by wandering roaches or outright spies, groups of grasshoppers would be allowed to roam across the area between the dairying colony and the fire ant colony for hunting purposes. Catches of plastic would be concealed in thickets of tall grasses to be found by the dairying ants. Delegations had left in two directions to sister fire ant colonies. The colony's chief tunnel engineer had already begun a tunnel to the dairying colony. It would be wide enough in the beginning for two ants to pass for trade, and be expanded to a four-ant width as soon as they had the hoped-for volunteer workers from their sister colonies.

Fauna figured the two dairying ants she was with now felt the same sort of confusion along with happiness that she did. Their whole world was changing, too. She sensed they wanted to talk about it, but that would simply have to wait. Maybe while they camped overnight....

Fane returned. "I found a place we can hide close to a field latrine. I saw them come there during their mid-day meal break," he said. "Stay low and follow me."

Fane led them in a wide circle around a place where the harvester ants were turning over the soil to prepare for spring planting. One tuft of the tall grassfronds from the previous season cycle remained on the edge of the field, concealing an outdoor latrine. This consisted of a piece of wood with two abdominal-sized holes in it, covering a pit below.

Once in place, Fane whispered to the other three, "I'm going to hide myself in the tall grass of the latrine. One of those harvesters working in the soil will have to come eventually. I'll reach from behind and hold their mandibles closed, so whomever we encounter won't shout an alarm. As soon as I do, Dailey and Dagan, you must get up enough for them to see you and signal for silence. Then I can whisper only the most needed words. Dagan, you hold out the letters. I noticed that the workers had satchels, so whomever we catch can hide the letters from both our councils to read later. I'll whisper a place to bury the box I've been carrying in my satchel in which future communications will be placed."

They all nodded to each other and settled down to wait for one of the harvester ants to need to use the latrine. Fane was hoping a male would approach first, but in the middle of the afternoon, it was a female harvester who came. Knowing he would probably startle her, Fane let her settle over the hole before he wrapped his middle pods around her and clamped his front pods over her mandibles. "Hush," he whispered.

The female harvester's breath came in quick gasps, but she did not struggle against Fane's grip.

Dailey and Dagan rose and signaled quiet. Dagan held out a sealed parchment. "Please, don't be afraid," Fane whispered. "We come as friends. I only grabbed you because you must not cry out so those roaches hear you. Can you be silent?"

At a weak nod from the female, Fane let go of her mandibles and loosened his hold her about the thorax. "What is your name?"

"I...am...Haley," she whispered back.

"I'm sorry I frightened you so, but it was necessary. I am Fane, and those standing before you are Dailey and Dagan—from the colony you were trading with. My partner Fauna is concealed next to them. We have a plan to free you from these roaches. We dare not talk very long now, but put those letters to your council in your satchel."

Haley nodded. She wasn't shaking as much now.

Fauna finally revealed her presence. Haley jumped again, but managed not to cry out. Fane stepped around in front of her. He whispered again, "We truly are sorry that we had to catch you at such a private moment, but I could think of no other way. You must not stay long. Go back now, but tell one of the others to come soon and not to be afraid or shout out."

"All...right; I'm all right, now...really," Haley whispered back as she stuffed the letters into her satchel. She lowered her head, took a few deep breaths to regain her composure, and headed back to the field.

A quarter h-unit later, a male approached. He seemed more ready for an encounter. Dagan and Dailey rose right away.

"I am Hal," he whispered, "and I recognize you two. Our roach masters took your baskets last time frame. I'm sorry we couldn't warn you—we tried. Why are you back? Haley said some hard-to-believe things—that two fire ants were here."

Dagan made a sign for quiet and then Fane and Fauna rose from their hiding places. Hal's eyes widened but he did not shout out.

"We come in peace and friendship," Fauna whispered. "Haley has important letters in her satchel that will explain everything." She held out a small wooden box. We are going to bury this box right next to your latrine pit," she walked quickly to the spot they had chosen. "Put your communications to us in this box before this same day next time frame. We will take your news and leave more information. We will try not to see you directly unless you ask us to."

"All right," Hal whispered back.

"I remember you, too, Hal, from last time frame. We have many questions," Dagan said in a hushed voice, "but we don't want to attract attention, so all the information is in the letters. You should go back to the field now."

"Do you want Haley to come again?"

"Not today," Fauna said. "But we will be here again tomorrow morning so you can tell us your council chief's response."

They all nodded to each other. Hal headed back to the field and the other four ants sank back into hiding.

Council Chief Hesper stared at Haley in disbelief as she told of her encounter with their trading partners and the fire ants who had accompanied them. But when Hesper broke the seal and read the first letter, her mandibles opened so wide that one of the slender variety roaches might have crawled between them:

From: Dahlia, Council Chief of your
        Dairying Ant Trade Partners
        Second Time Frame 25, in a
        New Season Cycle of Hope
To: Our Harvester Friends

I know that this may seem unbelievable to you at first, but we have a plan to free you from the roaches who have taken over your colony. This has come about because of the desperation of a sister dairying colony of ours a long day's journey to the north. They have been enslaved by roaches for many season cycles. At first, these roaches allowed them to continue life as usual, but then a much harsher roach came to be in charge and has deprived them of plastic for their young, who are now dying of extreme plastic deprivation. One of their members managed to escape and came to us for help. About this same time, our spiritual guide had a dream from Essence of the unification of all ants. In the last quarter time frame, we have joined with a fire ant colony between us and our sister dairying colony. They are now supplying our plastic needs and we are providing them with food. They will be the force that will free you and our sister colony. Their spiritual guide and the other dairying colony's spiritual guide had the same dream of the unification of all ants.

I must leave out many details for now, but we will be building a tunnel from our colony to yours, from our colony to our fire ant friends, and from the fire ant colony to the other dairying colony. The invasion to free you will come through that tunnel near the end of this season cycle. We will keep you informed of progress each time frame so you will know the day and hour and be ready for it.

We and the fire ant colony are reaching out to other colonies we know of for help in this endeavor. We hope to reach out to colonies beyond those as well to form a "colony of colonies" *to share our knowledge and skills and provide protection for each other.*

We need help from you as well. First, will you provide us with a map of your colony so we may plan the best place for our tunnel to enter? Second, do the roaches who control you have an interpreter? If so, you must be very careful not to let that roach overhear anything about these plans. Third, is it possible for those who brought you this letter to return to the field tomorrow with a preliminary answer from you? Also, are you still provided plastic for your young? If you are, we urge you to instruct all adults to stop consuming their shares of plastic and hide extra supplies within your homes in the event that the roaches may suddenly decide to stop giving you plastic—as they did with our sister colony. Our sister colony also advises you to set up a quiet communication system between all colony members that the roaches will not know about. Our sister colony set up a system like this: One ant memorizes the message and passes it to five or six others with whom that ant works, or near whom they live; these then memorize the message and pass it to five or six more, until all have heard the message.

The party of dairying ants and fire ants who contacted you today will come again in the same manner in the morning and on the same day of the third time frame to bring you more news and get more detailed answers from you.

> *Your compassionate friend in Essence,*
> *Dahlia Dairier*

Hesper laid down the letter and lowered her head. The second letter was similar but signed by the Fire Ant Council Chief.

"Are you all right?" Haley asked.

A moment went by before Hesper replied. "For a moment, I felt as if I had been struck by lightning, but yes, I'm all right. Everything will be all right now." She handed the first letter to Haley. When Haley had finished reading it, Hesper said, "Hadi came to me this morning and told me that he had the same dream—all ants together! He was confused about the meaning of the dream."

It was Haley's turn to stare in shock.

Hesper ran one front pod across her mandibles and to the tip of her antennae. "Haley, would you please go to Hadi's domicile and ask him to come to me?"

"Of course!"

"And in the morning, tell those who came to you that we welcome their help. I'll let you know more when you return with Hadi."

Fauna, Fane, Dagan, and Dailey retreated about a d-unit from the harvester colony. Fane chose a place about a quarter d-unit away from the trail near a grove of wood plants. Enough brush lay on the ground beneath the trees to form a rough shelter for the night.

"We may speak softly here," Fauna said, "but we must not have fire or any light at all."

While they ate and drank from their supplies, the four talked about their respective homes and families. All were somewhat surprised to learn that the two species had more traditions in common than they thought. The sun dipped below the horizon and darkness fell.

"All this time," Dagan said, "we thought you were our enemies. We've been so wrong."

"It's easy to understand that," Fauna said. "But I'm glad we are now friends. Fane, I'll take the first watch."

"The first what?" Dailey asked.

"One of us must guard the others through the night. Didn't you say that those who watch the grasshoppers at night keep watch?"

"Oh, yes, of course. But being carriers, it's been a long time since either of us stayed awake all night."

Fane nodded as Fauna climbed up one of the wood plants to get the best view. "It's all right. Both of you sleep well. Fauna will wake me halfway through the night. We are used to sleeping at all times of the day and being awake at all times of the night. It's part of our training."

It seemed as if no time had passed before daylight arrived. The group chewed quietly on dried grasshopper meat and drank more honeydew.

"Let's go see if Hal and Haley are back in the field. I'll lead. Silence again, please," Fane said.

Shadows were still long when they reached the field latrine and hid themselves as they had the previous afternoon. They watched the ants working in the field but none approached the latrine. Around midmorning, they sensed roach warriors. They froze in their places, hardly daring to breathe. Finally, the last of the roaches had taken care of their business at the latrine and they returned to watching over the ant workers.

Another full h-unit passed before Hal approached the latrine. He signaled quiet as he plopped his abdomen over the hole. A moment later he reached into his satchel and removed a sealed parchment. Fane rose slightly from hiding. The two ants nodded at each other. Fane reached out and took the letter.

In perfect silence, Fane showed Hal where the messages would be hidden in the future. The two males joined front pods in the gesture all ants used both in greeting and parting. Hal returned to the field to work. The other four ants retreated slowly in silence. Their mission successful, they returned to the dairying colony with good news.

21.

First Time Frame, 296 C.C.I.,
Henry Roach-Dairier II

I was grateful that South Harvester Colony 45's records were so complete. Every original letter from what became South Dairy 50 had been preserved, along with a copy of the letters they had sent. In addition, Hesper and Haley had both kept journals. And of course, Fire Ant 2 had also preserved their records. Between those two sets, it was possible for me to formulate an accurate account of what took place between the three colonies. Essence seemed to guide my thoughts when it came to the possible feelings of the dairying ants since there was a total absence of records from South Dairy 50, later lost to a different kind of disaster. South Dairy Colony 1 had also preserved all communications received and sent during that period. In several places, I decided it seemed more appropriate to quote the letters than to try to tell those parts of the story in my own words.

On my own home front, I received a message from my mother that Sir Rastus had requested a half-time-frame postponement of his suit against me. I had a little more time to prepare (and my mother was able to complete other pressing cases) before I had to face him and the Chief Enforcer. My mother's comment was, "It seems he's hired his own archeologist to do a little digging first."

Near the End of Second Time Frame, 1 B.C.C. and into the Next Several Time Frames

To: Our Dairying Friends
From: Hesper, Harvester Colony Council Chief
        Second Time Frame

You cannot imagine our dismay at learning what the roaches have done to others, or our joy at knowing that help is on its way to us, even though we had not yet sought it. The very day your news arrived, our spiritual guide, Hadi, reported to me his dream of all ants together—saying he did not understand the meaning of the dream. It is now clear to both of us.

The roach warriors here do not bother us much after the work day has ended, but as a precaution, after Hadi and I talked, I quietly convened a meeting of our council in my home rather than in Council Chamber.

The roaches who enslave us still allow our shares of plastic, adult as well as young. They have, however, emptied our central storage chamber of a season cycle's supply of plastic, so your warning to hide supplies is well given. We are developing a communications system like the one you described and will use it shortly to begin saving plastic supplies in our homes. If we do not need to use those supplies, we can put them back in our central storage chamber once we are free.

We do not have a roach who speaks our language, and at this point, if asked, we will not train one to do so. However, knowing that some roaches apparently do speak our language, we think it prudent to make sure none of our members discuss our communications with you when any roaches are around.

Our surface workers are not always in the same fields around our colony, but for the sake of future communications, we will make sure that Hal and Haley always have some sort of work to do in the field where you met them for the purpose of putting letters in the buried box and retrieving those you send.

It will take us several days to make a complete map of our colony. We will send that to you next time frame. For the time being, begin to build the tunnel beneath the surface trail you have been using.

> *Yours in Essence,*
> *Hesper, Colony Council Chief*

To: *South Dairy Colony 1*
From: *South Dairy Colony 50*
              Middle of Fourth Time Frame

To all our friends who suffer so:

Thank you for the map of your colony you sent last time frame. The fire ant commander is studying it to find the best entry point. We are glad to know the size of the roach force we will face. The feeling is 500 will be an easy number to defeat. As you see by our letter head, we are happy to begin using your colony name under the Combined Colonies of Insectia. You may also note that we have chosen the name South Dairy Colony 50. The harvester colony chose the name South Harvester Colony 45. We at this latitude have chosen to include "South" in our names because we have learned there are many of our species in northern climates, and far to our west as well—and harvester colonies, too. There may be colonies to the east, but Roacheria lies in the way of explorations for the time being. However, it seems our fire ant friends live only in these southern areas.

You will be gratified to know that the total number of colonies is now at fifteen, and more are joining us each quarter time frame! Each colony we meet knows of two or three more. Food and workers are pouring in from nearly 100 d-units away already. We and Fire 2 have built entrances at the back of our mounds where these arrivals are less visible to any wandering roaches. Scouts from Fire 2 watch closely night and day. Work on the tunnels is going twice as fast—also night and day. At this rate, we will be ready to free you sometime during Eleventh Time Frame. An exact date will be chosen as we get closer.

Even though we know you are still losing new young adults, and grieving for them, take heart. Your freedom grows closer with each h-unit.

> Yours in Essence,
> Dahlia, Council Chief

To: *South Harvester Colony 45*
From: *South Dairy Colony 50*
         End of Fourth Time Frame

To Our Friends:

Thank you for the colony map, which is being studied by the fire ant commander for the best entry point. Also, thank you for choosing your colony name and letting us know the number of roaches currently in your colony. We know you will inform us if this should increase for any reason.

We now have twenty colonies in the alliance. Workers are pouring in from over 100 d-units away. Some of them are actually helping excavate homes and dormitories that they can live in while they help us to free you. This will happen sometime during Eleventh Time Frame.

Please let Hal and Haley know how much we appreciate the risk they take with every delivered message.

Yours in Essence,
Dahlia, Council Chief

Duncan's life now seemed rather dull—the same route every day, the same check-in with Rashad at midday. He did, however, look forward to each time frame's communication with the "outside world" because he had been sending and receiving personal letters from Dara. Every night he read and reread the letters he had received. Even though he had to wait a time frame for the answer to any particular question, and their "conversations" seemed disjointed because of the lag times, he treasured what he received. He sensed the same caring in her letters that he tried to say to her. Early on, he had told her he felt inadequate because she had so much more training than he did. Her reply was that he couldn't help that and that when they could really spend time together, she would be happy to help him catch up.

Duncan began to hurry through his workday so he would have more time to read each evening. When the roaches had closed the training centers and the colony's research and reading center, the volumes had been split up among many homes. When Duncan had gone through all the books his parents had, be began to borrow from the homes of friends. Master Daeira had an extensive library as well and welcomed him any time.

During Sixth Time Frame, Duncan said to his spiritual guide, "I know you said to take my time deciding, but I feel more and more that I want to have a family. I hope it will be with Dara, but if not, I want to find someone else. I know now that I can't choose to be single as you did. But part of me also feels the call to continue to study with you."

She embraced him. "I understand. However, even though I, and spiritual leaders in our colony before me, chose not to mate, it was our choice. Recent communications from other colonies tell me that many spiritual guides in other colonies do have families."

"Really? Then I don't have to give up one to have the other?"

"That is correct. Please, continue to meditate on how best to serve your colony."

"I will. I promise."

To: South Dairy 1 and South Harvester 45
From: Dahlia, South Dairy 50
*   Seventh Time Frame*

Good news, my friends:

We now have over sixty colonies in The Combined Colonies of Insectia! Some of them are more than half a time frame's travel away and they are reaching out to others that are hundreds of d-units farther away. We are in constant communication with new colonies every day. The amount of time it takes to get messages back and forth is sometimes frustrating, but we are adjusting to incredible changes to our lives.

Both tunnels are now over half way completed—at four ants wide! The most difficult part is hauling all the excavated dirt and rock long distances back to our colony and Fire 2 to be added to the tops of our mounds rather than having multiple entrances to the surface along the way. Small side chambers have been built at intervals so workers can sleep and eat near the newest diggings. Many volunteers are involved in just transporting food and other supplies to the digging and taking soil back along the completed tunnel. Please lift up your thoughts to Essence for our wonderful tunnel engineers who are working so hard. Ask Essence to give them extra energy for the task.

These tunnel engineers now feel confident that we will reach both of you by the middle of Eleventh Time Frame. Commander Fadi and his captains are working with nearly 2000 fire ants from fifteen different colonies to coordinate the attack plans. We should have complete details to you by the beginning of Tenth Time Frame.

Yours in Essence,
Dahlia

Firstday, First Time Frame, 21, 329 O.R. (296 C.C.I.)
Henry Roach-Dairier II

The hearing chamber was crowded and clearly divided between our supporters and those who agreed with Sir Rastus—on respective sides of the chamber with a row of warrior-trained enforcers standing between them and all around the sides of the chamber. This was due to several episodes of violence in the streets of Roacheria during the two previous days. Several roaches had been standing in front of Sir Rastus' city mansion and shouting out that he should stop persecuting me. I didn't personally know these roaches, and I did not condone their actions, but it felt good to know that so many agreed with what I was doing.

Sir Rastus had sent out his personal warriors, telling them, "Remove them from my property!" Several of those shouting were injured. The following day, even more turned out—with a few warrior friends of their own. It took about a hundred enforcers to end the riot. No one knew for sure how many were injured.

The eyes of those against me bored into me like iron spikes into soft wood. My supporters and my mother looked at me with softness in an attempt to help keep me calm. The Chief Enforcer's eyes held skepticism. Sir Rastus' counselor-of-law's eyes were the most intimidating of all. I tried to focus on my mother, but I had to look at the counselor while being questioned.

My mother had prepared me the best she could, including reminding me at least half-a-dozen times that she could not speak or object during that part of the questioning. It was up to me to remember everything she had told me.

"So, you wish to dig for archeological evidence of some ant colony that nobody ever heard of, based on an old journal entry. Is that correct?"

"Yes," I answered.

"Why?"

"If evidence of this colony is found, we wish to place a memorial marker there."

"Why?" Sir Rastus' counselor persisted.

"For pretty much the same reason that roaches place memorial markers at the place where their cherished ones are covered—that they may not be forgotten."

"And you want nothing more? No monetary gain? Whom do you expect to pay for this outrageous project?"

"To the first question, no. To the second, no. To the third, the expenses of the dig and the memorial marker, if evidence of the colony is found, will be paid for by private donations."

"Who are these donors?"

"I believe the word 'private' covers that."

A ripple of laughter rose on our side of the chamber.

"How much have you received?"

"Nothing, as yet. I have promises from donors after I have secured permission for the dig. I believe all this information was presented in the proposal for the dig. That has already been entered into evidence in this hearing."

"Yes, it has, as has the testimony from a well-known archeologist that he's seen no evidence on the surface of anything."

That was true enough—on both counts. Sir Rastus' "expert" had stated that the surface was quite flat—no evidence of a bump, hill, or such as would still be seen of an ant colony—including the fact that "Old South Dairy 50's" mound was a prominent part of the landscape so there couldn't have been a colony.

My mother had refuted this theory with her expert's evidence that if a mound were intentionally torn down and smoothed over the surface, different soils would be on the top compared to the surrounding area. Soil that came from tunnels deep underground would have been at the top of the mound and then spread over an area where other surface soil would be. It had been an impressive demonstration with a model of a colony using sands of different shades and textures of soil just as it would be in a real colony. She had also gotten Sir Rastus' archeologist to admit he had done absolutely no soil testing, or even put a shovel to the earth.

Rabiah had been called to testify about how I had approached her. So had the chief librarian concerning the maps. Both had been strongly in my favor and had withstood Sir Rastus' counselor's onslaught of questions intended to upset them and trip up their testimony.

"Your next question," I prodded. This was followed by snickers from some of those watching the proceedings—a few of them from Sir Rastus' supporters.

"And you don't think all this has reflected, or will reflect, negatively on my client, especially with the events of the last few days?"

I answered his question with another question. "Why should it?"

"I'll ask the questions here! We've seen more than negative statements made in public. Chief Enforcer, I believe I've made that clear. I would ask you now to rule in our favor."

The Chief Enforcer looked down on Sir Rastus and his counselor from his high bench. "Considering the fact that some of the violence of late has supposedly been for your client, I can't see that you've proved your point. According to law, a Roacherian Citizen today is not responsible for the possible actions of his or her roachcestors. If you have no more questions for this young male, I'll excuse him."

"I have more questions, Chief Enforcer."

"Then, please, ask them."

Sir Rastus' counselor shuffled through some papers in front of him and then asked, "Isn't your intent—in trying to prove this supposed colony existed—to state so in some book you purport to write?"

"If a scientific dig shows this colony did exist, then I will include that fact in my account of the events prior to the formation of The Combined Colonies of Insectia and why the colonies united at that time. If a scientific dig shows no evidence, then I will not put any mention of said non-existing colony in my account. I seek only to verify that such a colony did, or did not exist."

"And you guarantee that my client's good name will not be tarnished?"

"I can't guarantee how anyone might regard the ancient Sir Ragnar's actions. Public opinion is what it is. I have no control over that. Nor do you, or anyone here. My purpose has always been to promote the truth about those days so that we, today, might reflect upon the past in a different way, understanding it more clearly and seeing how it has affected our thoughts and opinions so we might change those opinions as we desire. As has been stated, Sir Rastus cannot, and should not, be held in any way responsible for what his roachcestors may have done. If there have been negative comments in public of late, perhaps they result from his refusal to allow the truth to come to light."

"Lord Chief Enforcer, do you see how his very comment now disparages my client?" Both the counselor and Sir Rastus looked as if they might explode in anger. More than quiet comments echoed about the chamber.

"Silence!" demanded the Chief Enforcer. Regular enforcers who stood around the sides of the chamber moved toward the most vocal in order to escort them out. Those removed had all been seated on Sir Rastus' side of the chamber.

When the chamber had quieted down, the Chief Enforcer continued. "That's better. I'll rephrase your question for you, counselor. Henry, what actions will you take to minimize such negative public opinions?"

Now I was back on the spot. I outlined the steps my mother and I had discussed. "I have already taken many steps. You have seen the number of letters I wrote asking Sir Rastus to speak with me about any information he might have in his possession—just as I did with the descendants of Sir Rainart, which led to a much more favorable impression of Sir Rainart to be presented in my published account. You have seen that my letters were refused and returned. You have heard Sir Rastus, under questioning from my counselor, admit that he slammed the portal in my face. These were all steps on my part to try to ensure less negative reaction. Sir Rastus' own actions have resulted in the comments about him so far. I have stated here, and in writing, that Sir Rastus will have income from the sale of any artifacts that might be found. He has the right to charge an admission fee onto his surface area should he wish to. I actually hope that we find no evidence of a colony there."

I did not state out loud that I found the idea of what may have happened there to be so horrific that I didn't want to face the fact that an outright slaughter of innocent creatures could have taken place. I continued with, "I seek forgiveness in advance from Sir Rastus for anything I may have said, or done, that would disparage his family today. I would proclaim these publicly, and indeed am doing so now. I hold nothing against his family today."

That was the center point of the entire matter. Public opinion in the streets of Roacheria had been much against Sir Rastus in the last half time frame. Many educated roaches spoke out against him in and outside the SERCB chambers because of his refusal to allow the dig and his suit against me. Even more had asked my mother and me what I had been working on so she had found it necessary to make a public statement about my research into those early times. Excitement was high as those in the streets speculated about what my book would say. Hundreds of advance orders had poured in to my mother's office— orders which came from both "sides" of the issue.

The next words I said did not seem to come from myself, and I remembered how my grandfather had once had a similar experience. "If Sir Rastus still feels I have wronged him, then let him set a monetary demand, and I will pay it, even if it takes me a lifetime of working in his service to do so. If he so desires, all income from the sales of copies of my work may go to him. But I cannot guarantee what others might say, or think about him, due to his actions and words. I would urge my fellow citizens of Roacheria to behave in a civilized manner at all times. Like my grandfather and his grandfather, I do not believe in violence to solve disagreements. I am willing to serve, and lay down my own life if need be, for what I believe. Most of all, I do not condone the violence of the last few days. I would never participate in something like that, nor encourage others to do so."

My mother's mandibles opened in shock at my words along with those of nearly everyone in the chamber. I had basically given Sir Rastus his "victory" in my willingness to become his servant or be sent to the mantis compound at his command if the Chief Enforcer ruled in his favor.

The Chief Enforcer raised a pod for silence before any ruckus could begin again. He addressed the chamber. "I believe I've heard everything I need to in order to render a decision—which I will do in two days. I could announce it now, but because of the extreme emotions present in this chamber and elsewhere, I shall wait for the citizens of Roacheria to calm down before doing so. Fellow enforcers, I charge you to keep the peace in the streets as this chamber empties. And I warn all citizens that further violence in the streets will result in a lot of fat mantises. We are adjourned."

The Chief Enforcer rose and left the chamber through his own exit.

22.

Editorial Comments,
Henry Roach-Dairier II, 296 C.C.I.

By Ninth Time Frame of that antstoric season cycle, 1 B.C.C., the number of colonies in the new Combined Colonies of Insectia had reached 100. Their area extended approximately 800 d-units north and 800 d-units west of South Dairy 50 and Fire 2. Since there were plans to continue to reach out to even more distant colonies, a harvester colony to the northeast near the convergence of the Great East-Flowing and Great South-Flowing rivers where there was a vast area of Duo Pod ruins and plastic mines, agreed to become the home of the Intercolonial Council, a "council of councils" for the "colony of colonies." It took the name Central Harvester 12—"twice the number of our pods to symbolize the multiplication of our strengths in the new Combined Colonies of Insectia."

This seems a good place to note why modern ants and roaches came to live in specific areas of the greater land mass we occupy. Ants covered a much larger geographic area because of their ability to tunnel under rivers too wide to cross easily. During those early days, roaches lacked the technological ability to build extensive bridges. They weren't much good at building vessels to cross the rapidly flowing waters either, so they were limited to the area east of the Great South-Flowing River that splits this land mass pretty much in half. They were also confined to the area south of the Great West-Flowing River that emptied into the Great South-Flowing River, so that "East Roacheria" ranged through the south-east quadrant of the land mass. "South Roacheria" began west of the Great South-Flowing River and mingled in places with the ant colonies.

The two species kept pretty much to themselves for hundreds and hundreds of season cycles until some roaches attempted to devise a bridge of rafts across the Great South-Flowing River to combine the two areas of Roacheria. The cost of this bridge had been provided by Sir Rainart, and resulted in Sir Rainart's economic desperation and his idea to "manage" South Dairy Colony 1. Sir Rainart did manage to influence the various cities and towns of South Roacheria to unite under the South Roach Control Board, but the bridge and the combining of the South and East Roacheria both failed. The two areas of Roacheria did not manage to combine until a few generations later, at which point the City of Roacheria did become the center of government, in spite of the fact that it was so far to the western edge of Roacheria, and therefore not "central" at all.

Perhaps Central Harvester 12 being the home of the Intercolonial Council lacked a similar kind of logic, because once the Combined Colonies were all set and together, Central Harvester 12 was about as far from "central" to all the colonies (well, it is "central" in terms of north and south) as the City of Roacheria was "central" to all the Roacherian cities and smaller communities. I suppose the roach leaders hoped they could expand forever westward and early ant leaders hoped they might find even more ant colonies to their east, which would have put both governing bodies truly in the "center." That might have been the case if the two species had somehow managed to continue to leave each other alone. It occurs to me that if Sir Ragnar had listened to Rashad and let the ants have their much-needed plastic, and if some other unknown board member had not set his greedy eyes on South Harvester 45, things might have been very different.

Tenth Time Frame, 1 B.C.C.

To: South Dairy Colony 1
From: Fire Colony 2
Tenth Time Frame

Council Chief Delana and all colony members:

The invasion for your freedom will begin on the 15th day of Eleventh Time Frame at 6:00 h-units in the morning. The 1,000 guards who will free you will be camped in the tunnel overnight so that they are rested and ready. You must instruct all colony members not to start their work day early. All must remain in their domiciles until the guards under Captain Farr call through the tunnels that it is safe to come out.

They will hear things that may frighten them, but they are not to worry. When the guards pour through your colony's tunnels moving upward, our defense cry will echo with them. It is a high-pitched whine mixed with a clicking noise that we emit by rapidly rubbing our outer mandibles against each other—it is meant to be frightening. You will probably hear the roaches yell as we engage them in battle. They will also wail loudly as our venom kills them. You must not let these sounds disturb you.

After the roaches have been defeated, we will call through the tunnels to tell you all is safe. We are anxious to meet you in person and begin to celebrate. Captain Farr and most of the guards will remain with you permanently, helping you to rebuild your colony and keeping you safe from any possibility that roaches might try to invade you again. All fire ant guards are trained in colony jobs as well as in defensive tactics, so many will fill in your work force as needed while others patrol your surface boundaries day and night.

The families of those guards who are mated will come to live with them as soon as it is possible. Other varieties of ants will come later as volunteers to live and work with you in any needed area. We have the distinct impression that many nursery workers will be needed about four time frames after you are free. We also understand that many different types of trainers will be wanted to fill in the training gaps of your young adults—even though they may be parents themselves and working around the colony while they strive to learn subjects they were deprived of under the control of the roaches. A secondary goal of the new Combined Colonies of Insectia will be for young adults to travel freely between colonies sharing culture, traditions and knowledge, and inter-mating between different kinds of ants.

Yours in Essence,
Commander Fadi

Tenth Time Frame

My most-cared-for Duncan,

I want to tell you that I've placed my name at the very top of the list for voluntary migration to your colony, and I have been approved! That is how much I want to be near you and be able to spend much more time getting to know you. I think I was approved because of our friendship as much as because of my broad training—I can be assigned to almost any work area where someone is needed, and I am single, so I don't have to move with a mate and young ones. I hope you do not think me forward for doing this without discussing it with you by letter first. I am counting the days.

Your caring and hoping-to-be-more-than friend,
Dara

Duncan held the letter closely to his thorax. He sat down and wrote his reply—only one more sending of messages would occur on the first of Eleventh Time Frame when his colony let Commander Fadi know all would be ready. Duncan began to count not just the days but the hours.

To: *South Harvester 45*
From: *Fire Colony 2*
        Tenth Time Frame

Council Chief Hesper and all colony members:

The invasion for your freedom will begin on the 15th day of Eleventh Time Frame at 6:00 h-units in the morning. ...

(Editorial note: The two letters were essentially the same except for parts of the last paragraphs—H.R-D-II, 296 C.C.I.)

Once the roaches have been driven from your colony, I will return to my home. Most of the guards will remain with you, patrolling your surface area day and night, constantly on the watch to defend you against any return of the roaches. Captain Fleur, my assistant, will be in command of all the guards. She will manage their schedules and work closely with everyone in your colony. All fire ant guards are trained in colony jobs as well as defense, so many will work in any area from refuse collection to the building of new domiciles and tunnels as needed. We hope volunteers from your colony will decide to migrate to our colony, temporarily or permanently, as we very much want to learn the skills of growing seeds and other useful plants in which your members specialize. A secondary goal of the new Combined Colonies of Insectia will be for young adults to travel freely between colonies sharing culture, traditions and knowledge, and inter-mating between different kinds of ants.

Your servant in Essence,
Commander Fadi

The Day of Freedom:
South Harvester Colony 45,
the First of the Two Simultaneous Battles

Hal and Haley did not sleep much the night before the 15th day of Eleventh Time Frame. They were probably not the only ants awake that night. The hours dragged as they waited for 6:00 h-units. They had finished breakfast by 5:00 h-units and paced about their domicile. Both listened from time to time near the portal of their "oldest" young one's pupation chamber, since that daughter was due to emerge as an adult any day. The other pupation chambers in their domicile would be silent for another two and four season cycles.

Finally, 6:00 h-units arrived.

"Shouldn't we have heard something by now?" Haley asked at 6:10.

Hal shook his head. "We are close to the surface and they will enter at the lowest level. Sound doesn't carry that well." He circled his mate with his front pods to try to calm her.

In another ten moments, they began to hear it. It did not seem high-pitched at first, distant as it was, and softened by layers of earth between the levels of the colony. But as the sound grew louder, the pitch seemed to increase. Shouts in Roach with the urgency of an alarm came from their own tunnel. The pods of roach warriors thumped along the floor outside their portal—a good many roach warriors occupied domiciles along that residential tunnel.

The two ants who had risked so much over the last several time frames without apparent fear now clung to each other. They could hear a jumble of roach voices very close—disjointed shouting as if in chaos. Then the real terror of the battle reached them. The Fire Ant Battle Cry was indeed frightening. Even though they had been told not to worry, Hal and Haley pushed their heavy cooking box against the portal to prevent anyone from entering. Then they ran into their sleep chamber as far from their portal as possible, pressing their heads together with the thought that blocking at least one hearing organ each, the sounds of battle would diminish. It didn't help. Moments dragged by.

Screams and moans vibrated through their portal.

Desperate sounds: cries, screams, wails, pounding pods in the floor and walls of the tunnel.

Exoskeletons thumped against their portal.

Then gradually, the sounds diminished. The Fire Ant Battle Cry moved on beyond their tunnel and the portal to their domicile, and upward toward the colony's main entrance.

It seemed like half a day had passed, but it was barely 7:00 h-units when they heard the triumphant cries of the Fire Ant Guards.

"Come out! Come out! It is safe. You are free!"

Hal shoved the cooking box back from the portal, and then Haley opened it with shaking pods. Dozens of roach bodies lay along the tunnel. Fire ants were beginning to carry away the dead. Their neighbors emerged and they greeted each other, embracing and expressing their relief after the fearful h-unit.

One of the fire ants addressed them. "Are you all right?"

The harvester ants nodded.

"I'm sorry that you had to experience this. The roaches happened to choose this tunnel to make their final defense. You heard the very worst of it."

Hal found his voice. "Did many of you die?"

"There are many injuries that I am aware of, but to my knowledge, not a single ant life has been lost."

"What will you do with their bodies?" Hal asked.

"We will take them to the edge of your surface area and leave them for the flies—fly larva must eat, too. They will be a sign to other roaches of what will happen to them if they attack this colony again.

In my father's younger days, when they tried to attack our colony, we let pieces of their exoskeletons mark our surface boundaries and they have not attacked us since."

"How can we ever thank you?" Haley asked.

"No thanks are needed. We are all ants together now. We shall celebrate when this cleanup job is complete."

Joyful relief cruised through South Harvester 45. Members embraced each other in complete joy, caressing and stroking each other's thoraxes. Many ants wept. At midday, everyone brought forth freshly baked bread made from ground grassfrond seeds as well as roasted seeds, and ale made from fermented, mashed seeds. Hesper spread the word for the celebration to move onto the surface where there was room enough for all.

Ants came forward with their flutes made from the hollowed stems of the grassfrond plant—their primary product. Singing and dancing continued through the afternoon and into the evening.

23.

The Day of Freedom, South Dairy Colony 1:
The Second of the Two Simultaneous Battles

Captain Farr lay in the darkness. A thin layer of earth separated him from the lowest tunnel of South Dairy Colony 1. All of his guards kept the same total silence that the tunnel diggers had during the final week of construction—something that had actually delayed the tunnel's completion. They were all supposed to be sleeping so they would be ready for the charge at 6:00 h-units. He wondered how many of them were awake like he was. He knew at least two were—the last two who were to keep a dim lamp lit and in turns, watch the time, tapping those nearest them at fifteen moments before 6:00 h-units. He couldn't begin to count the number of times they had practiced this so when they tapped each other, someone who might have been in deep slumber would not cry out.

He let his mind go over—again—some of the words Commander Fadi had said yesterday before they left.

"None of us—in our lifetimes—have experienced the kind of battle you are going into. This is no beetle hunt. This is no surrounding of some stray roach, or even a few of them, whose organs of smell didn't seem to work to tell them they were on our surface. This will be a real battle. Many of you may be seriously injured or killed, as in the days of my parents, long before I even hatched, when a horde of roaches decided to try to take over our home.

"You outnumber them, and your venom is a much more effective weapon than their mandibles, but they will fight. They will try to kill you. Most of you have faced a mantis at one time or another. The mantis only kills for food. These roaches kill for no reason! You have the skills you need to defend yourselves and take them out. You must not hesitate to use your mandibles or sting them. This battle will

197

be a time to set aside compassion, or it will be you who die, your families who will mourn. Fix in your minds the suffering of South Dairy Colony 1. Focus on how you would feel if those were your larva withering in the sun, if those were your young adults dying of plastic deprivation. Those of you who will be with me at South Harvester Colony 45, you are fighting to prevent the same thing from happening there. Keep those young ones in your minds."

"Yes, Commander!" all had responded.

"If, and I doubt this will happen, the roaches should surrender without a fight, then you must show compassion. But stay on your guard against a trick! We've seen more than a few of them try to spy on us, pretend to leave, and then sneak back and try to attack us from behind. You've heard this from our sister colonies who live close to them, too. Do not trust them! Should you chase some from the colony and across the meadows, let those few escape. They will tell the tales of what happened to others, and that will serve as a deterrent to other roach warriors. We want them to fear us! That is the most important part of our defense—that they don't try to attack in the first place. Watch each other's thoraxes. May Essence be with us."

"Yes, Commander!" resounded through the chamber again.

Captain Farr's mind also recalled what Commander Fadi had said to him and Captain Fleur in private. "I have chosen the two of you to be in-residence commanders of our sister colonies because I believe you have zero trust in any roaches. It is good to trust our own, but better to be suspicious of all roaches. Never let yourselves become complacent if, after several time frames or season cycles, the roaches make no reappraisal attacks. Always be prepared to ward off attack. Don't lull your minds into thinking it won't happen, because that is exactly when it will."

To which both of them had said, "You can count on us, Commander."

Every guard under Farr's command had memorized the colony map. Every guard and unit (groups of twelve), along with their unit leaders, knew the pattern of tunnels they were to follow to the surface, splitting and uniting as needed so that every tunnel was cleared of roaches. They had practiced similar moves in the tunnels of their own colony. They had rehearsed the clicks and whistles they would use to call to those near them if they encountered a larger force of roaches while another unit found none. They were ready.

At some point, sleep did overcome Captain Farr, because the tap from the unit member nearest to him woke him. He tapped back his readiness and that tap spread through the guards. They rose, ready to charge. The timekeeper's final message came.

Captain Farr and three others plunged through the thin wall of earth and it collapsed. They began their wailing, clicking battle cry and tore along the tunnel.

The first roach warrior Captain Farr encountered did not even have time to cry out before Farr fell upon him, shoved his body to the side, and continued on. At the first tunnel junction, he and his units went to the right, others to the left in turn, keeping the numbers of ant guards balanced as they proceeded through the colony.

Not one dairying ant was about. They had followed their instructions exactly.

Halfway to the surface, the numbers of roaches began to increase and the fire ant guards came upon the first real resistance. Farr swung his abdomen to the right and left, stinging repeatedly at his foes; the others in his unit did the same. The looks on the faces of the roaches of shock, then fear, and then the wail before death was strangely satisfying. His thoughts—that's for the larva you left to wither; that's for the suffering of young adults—propelled him on. He had never been ruthless and in some ways was uncomfortable with the feeling, but that had to be set aside for now.

At first, he had counted the number of roaches he stung—six, then twelve, then…he lost count. Onward and upward. He didn't feel the least bit tired.

As the units had fanned outward through the lower and middle tunnels, some now began to come together again, since they all knew the largest numbers of roach warriors lived in one section near the colony's main entrance.

Five hundred fire ant guards, male and female, faced the rest of the roach warriors while the balance of fire ant guards cleared out the middle and upper level tunnels. Roach resistance at the junction of the tunnel into the roach domicile area and the wide tunnel leading to the colony's main entrance was fierce. Roach warriors poured out of their area into the midst of the fire ant guards lunging forward, slashing with their mandibles. All of these warriors were at least four times larger than the fire ants.

They stomped down their pods to crush the ants while biting at any part of an ant's body they could get hold of with their outer mandibles. Captain Farr crawled out from beneath a roach whose abdomen he had stung only to pounce on the back of the thorax of another who had pinned down one of his fellow guards.

"Onward! Push forward!" Captain Farr shouted.

The noise of the battle was deafening. The way it echoed through the tunnels seemed to amplify it. The odor of body fluids assaulted their antennae. Farr found it difficult to know whether or not they were winning. One of his middle appendages ached so badly he couldn't move it. He didn't even want to look.

Then from behind came new wails and clicks of the rest of the fire ant guards, their chore of clearing the mid-level tunnels complete.

Roach warriors, hearing the ant battle cry afresh, must have realized they had now lost their edge. Several broke ranks and ran for the surface. As fast as they did, other ants pursued them—Captain Farr hustling along on five legs less quickly than he could on six.

Farr singled out one roach to chase. The moment that roach turned to look back brought his doom. Farr went into a somersault that ended with his stinger in the very end of the roach's abdomen.

Four or five roach warriors continued to run, slipping away from the ants who ran after them.

Captain Farr looked around. The battle was over!

"Let them go," he shouted to those still chasing the roaches. The six ants stopped and turned back.

"Captain, your leg!" one said to him. "Let me call for a medical guard."

Captain Farr finally looked at his aching appendage. The last three segments were gone. Body juice dripped from the end. He slumped to the ground, grabbed some fallen leaves, and pressed them to the end of his middle-right appendage. "I'll be fine for now. See to others first. I need a casualty report, a roach body count, and start taking the roach bodies to the edge of the river as a warning to others. Let our friends know it is safe for them to come out."

Captain Farr looked at the angle of the sun—it seemed to be about 10:00 h-units. Then he fell to the ground.

Captain Farr woke up to see one of his unit assistants and a member of their medical team looking down at him.

"How'd I get here?"

"You lost consciousness, Captain. I carried you, but you're going to be fine," the medical guard said.

Farr looked at his middle appendage—swathed in bandages stained with his life juice. "The others? How long have I been out?" He tried to roll onto his side to rise.

His assistant pressed him down, gently moving him back onto the sleep cushion. "Please, Captain, lie back and rest. You are in good pods. It's three h-units past noon. We suffered thirty dead and nineteen injured. The roach body count was 494—so only six of them got away. Council Chief Delana checked every one of the bodies looking for Rashad, the interpreter. She did not find him, so we assume he was one of those who escaped. Delana would like to see you as soon as you are up to it."

Farr looked to the medic who nodded but said, "You may have visitors if you promise to stay on this cushion. You lost a lot of life juice; you are very weak right now."

A few moments later, a stately-looking female entered the medical center chamber.

"Captain Farr, I am so happy to meet you, and so saddened at your injury, and the loss of life among your guards. I am Delana," she said extending her front pods in greeting.

Farr took her pods gently in his. "Our losses are nothing—and much less than I expected actually—compared to what your colony has been through."

She nodded and then smiled. "This is a day of great joy for us, tempered by your losses. Words can't begin to express our thanks at what you and all the others have done for us today. Your assistant told us that your tradition is that a fallen guard should be covered where he or she fell, but we would not like to think they are trampled upon under the soil of tunnels where this battle took place. We would like to cover them with our own in the heart of our colony if that is all right with you."

Farr nodded.

"I would like to write to each one's family personally if I may," Delana said.

"Of course. I'll make sure you receive a list of names, since I'll need the same list for my own use."

"Now, to joyful things!" Delana continued. "I don't know if you are aware of it, but we have 102 pairs of young adults who have waited—some as long as fifteen season cycles—to be mated. We will have a huge mating ceremony tomorrow at noon, just outside the main entrance where there is room enough for all. We want all of you to join us in this celebration of hoped-for new life and our freedom."

The medic spoke up again. "Captain, if you promise to stay on a cushion—definitely no dancing for you—I'll carry you up there myself and tend to you, but if you won't promise that, I'll tie you down to this cushion and make sure you stay here."

Farr smiled. "I promise to stay on the cushion."

All of them laughed.

"It's been a long time since we had anything to laugh about," Delana said. "Captain Farr, or Commander, since the letter from your commander indicated that you would be staying with us as our guard commander, Master Daeira would like to meet you, too. But before then, I want you to know we have planned carefully for your guards to live in groups in the many empty domiciles around the colony until such time as we can arrange them in your customary manner."

"Thank you, and I suppose it is 'Commander'. I'll have to get used to that idea. Good thing I have assistants and captains to do patrol work now," he pointed to his bandaged appendage. "I am afraid my fighting days may be permanently over, but I'm still quite capable of managing and delegating duties to others." He turned to his assistant again. "Will you get me a list of all casualties, make a schedule for all uninjured guards: four-h-unit alternating shifts to patrol the areas along the river. During the celebration, arrange it so they switch off every two h-units so that all may participate in the celebration part of the time."

His assistant, soon to be named a captain, nodded and left the chamber. The others had all left to attend to other tasks when Master Daeira came in.

"Long have I waited for this day," she told him, "and I dreamed of you last night." She took both his front pods in hers and then stroked him gently while she looked deeply into his eyes. "I know your heart is troubled. Would you like to join me in meditation for a few moments?"

To Farr, Master Daeira looked as if she must be in her ninth decade of life. He was surprised later to learn she was only sixty-some season cycles in age. He began to understand the toll on her as she kept her colony's hope alive all those season cycles of slavery.

Both were silent for a moment before Farr nodded and said, "It's hard to say this, but I must. May Essence forgive my lust for killing this morning. I gave in to anger. That led to liking the fact that I was killing—an uncomfortable feeling for me. And that led to a careless abandon in my defense. The loss of part of my leg is the direct result of that carelessness."

"I know Essence understands your heart. Let it go now and be at peace with Her. None of us are perfect."

The two of them held each other's pods and meditated silently. Farr felt peacefulness pass through him, a great relief.

"I would think there may be more guards who might need to find peace in their hearts. How would you suggest I approach them?" Daeira asked.

Farr sighed. While he knew he needed to face his own anger, others might want to shove such feelings aside or deny that they felt them. "I'll have it announced that you are available. Some will come forward as I did. At first, it might be good if you had a group meditation session—or a series of them—which I'll have all guards attend. Once I've recovered enough, I'll plan to meet with each of my guards individually. I'll admit my own failings to help them open up; then I'll send some to you."

The dairy ants had six whole grasshoppers roasting slowly over pits of coals long before the sun rose. The aroma made everyone hungry. Other dairy colony members, with fire ant guards helping them, set up eating surface after eating surface and carried huge jugs of honey dew and fermented honeydew to the surface.

A medic carried Captain Farr on his cushion around half an h-unit before the ceremony, setting him down in a position to watch everything. Earlier that morning, Farr tried to stand on his own and had become dizzy. So he did not complain about staying on the cushion. Council Chief Delana and her family, Master Daeira, and Duncan soon joined him.

"Are you going to be all right?" Duncan asked Captain Farr.

"Absolutely! Sorry I couldn't get Dara here in time for this...."

Duncan smiled and then said, "I wouldn't want to rush into mating anyway. I would like to be able to enjoy a time of courtship. When will your family arrive?"

"Our oldest will emerge as an adult in about a time frame. My mate will come with her a few days after that. We have two others in various stages of pupation. Friends will watch over them, and one of us will go back about a quarter time frame before each is due to emerge and then bring them here a few days into their adulthood."

Just then, the families of the promised males and females began to come out of the colony into the middle of the gathering, carrying the adults about to be mated in baskets. It took the better part of an h-unit for the procession. In clusters of families, each male and female pledged himself or herself one to another and to their colony, with the colony pledging to support them as well. That part took place simultaneously. The babble of ant voices and the joy they expressed rang in Farr's head for many season cycles afterward.

Once the ceremonies were complete, the dancing, singing, and feasting lasted until after darkness fell. Farr tapped his back pods on the ground next to his cushion. Duncan offered him a mug of fermented honeydew, but he declined—wishing to set an example for those he commanded. Fire ant guards came and went, drinking only regular honeydew, watching for any signs of roaches who might try to mount a counter attack.

A full moon smiled down upon the celebrants on an unusually mild night for that time of the season cycle—so mild that it was safe for parents to take a few newly-hatched larva (who now would grow up normally, well supplied with plastic) out onto the surface in the pods of their happy parents, to join in the celebration. Wonderful song rose into the sky to the moon's smile—the "face of Essence."

Finally, families carried the newly-mated pairs in baskets to designated domiciles where they would spend a full quarter time frame together before returning to their respective jobs. Then all adults, except those on night duty with the grasshopper herds, retired. The work to rebuild South Dairy Colony 1 would begin early in the morning.

24.

First Time Frame 21, 329 O.R. (296 C.C.I.)
Henry Roach-Dairier II

"**W**hat were you thinking? Offering yourself to Sir Rastus!" my mother demanded to know once we were out of the Inquiry Chamber, but still in the Justice Center.

I stammered my reply. "Remember that time Grandfather... talked about not knowing what he was going to say and...feeling that his words were prompted by Essence? It was something like that. Everything just poured out. I hadn't planned that part. The same thing happened at Grandfather's covering."

Gabrielle sighed. "I know you have great faith in Essence, as do I. What I don't have is any respect for, or hope, that Sir Rastus will see it that way! I'm not sure about the Chief Enforcer either. And since your father.... I just couldn't take that again."

Mother was shaking. As I wrapped myself around her, she forced herself (as she often did) to recover her composure. My father, Ransom, had been murdered on the way back from the city to Meadow Common Wealth, two season cycles before, only two time frames after my mother was named to the SERCB. The murderers were caught—and sent to the mantis compound—but the pair never did reveal who had hired them. We all suspected it was someone on the Board who had opposed Mother's appointment. We supposed the act was meant to "encourage" her to resign, but it only made her more determined to continue.

A moment later, an enforcer we both knew approached. "Excuse me, Henry. Would you mind coming with me, please? The Chief Enforcer would like to meet with you privately."

"That's a bit outside protocol!" my mother snapped.

"I know," he replied, "but, please, come."

"Do I need my counselor with me?" I asked, referring to my mother.

"No, he asked for you—alone. Please, do not worry. You both know me, and you know I share your beliefs. I would never put you in danger, Henry."

Unsure of what to expect, I followed the enforcer through some back passages within the Justice Building and through an obviously little-known portal into the Chief Enforcer's private chamber. He rose as I entered the chamber and, unexpectedly, reached out with both front pods to greet me. I began to lower myself according to roach custom to acknowledge his power over me.

"No, not necessary," he said, extending both front pods again. "But I know that surprises you. Please, sit down."

I lowered my abdomen into a seat—the usual open-backed chair of Roacheria—but this one was so softly padded I felt as if I were sinking into it.

"There are certain pretenses I must keep up," the Chief Enforcer began, "and some feelings I must keep buried deep within my essence when I am out there on that judgment seat. I need to ask you a few things that could not be brought up in the public inquiry."

"Please, ask," I said, feeling more hopeful than I had a few moments before.

"Is it possible for me to read some of your work before we are both back in public?"

"I'm sorry, no. I left all of my research, notes, and draft in Fire Colony 2. Besides that, most of the draft is written in Ant, not Roach. But I'll be happy to tell you about it."

"I would appreciate that very much. By now, you must realize that my ruling will be in your favor. But I must choose my words carefully to appease Sir Rastus in some way, or I may set back all that I have accomplished in the name of Justice for the last several season cycles and in the future."

He turned to the enforcer, "Please tell Henry's mother that he will be a while, not to worry, and to go on home ahead of him."

Our enforcer friend nodded and left the chamber. He slipped back in a few moments later and listened in silence. I spent the next couple of h-units describing my work to the Chief Enforcer.

When I finally finished, the Chief Enforcer asked, "The donations you spoke of, those will come from the Combined Colonies, I assume."

"Some, yes, but I have many supporters here in Roacheria, too."

"Let it all come from roaches if possible," he said. "It sounds like the colonies have paid more than enough already, today and in the past."

"I'll have my mother put the word out."

"Good. Please, meditate on my behalf. I shall need the Wisdom of Essence when we are back in The Inquiry the day after tomorrow."

"I will do that. Thank you, more than you'll ever know."

"Our friend will escort you safely back to Meadow Commonwealth now."

I left his chambers wondering whether this had all been a dream.

Once back at Meadow Commonwealth, I told my family and the other commonwealth members over dinner about the private meeting. They found it almost impossible to believe that the Chief Enforcer was secretly an adherent of Antism. While many commonwealths existed in Roacheria, as a result of my grandfather's work, they consisted of mostly "working class" families. Very few roaches in positions of power, authority, or wealth had embraced the precepts of our way of life. My father, Ransom, was one of them—defying his father to give himself to my mother in mating and joining her to live at Meadow Commonwealth.

Parents in our group slipped quietly away to tend to their young ones while unattached adults remained in the Common Building to begin a special meditation session. We lifted up each other, the Chief Enforcer, and me, offering our thanks for what would come in two days and requesting the strength of Essence for true justice.

The main chamber at the Justice Center was even more crowded when we returned for the final ruling—especially the side of the chamber reserved for me and my supporters. Sir Rastus, his counselors, and clan numbered almost as many, filling their side of the chamber as well. A row of enforcers stood in the aisle separating us. It was so quiet that a piece of dandelion fluff would have echoed when it touched the floor.

The Chief Enforcer entered. Sir Rastus and I and our respective councilors rose to face him.

"It's quiet," he said. "Good. Let's keep it that way because I don't want to have to raise my pod for silence today. If I do, the creature or creatures causing the disruption won't like where I send them. So continue to keep your mandibles together."

All present in the chamber tipped antennae in a show of respect.

"As you are all well aware, there is usually a winner and a loser in this chamber. The loser pays—one way or another. But there is a precedent in our law allowing for a split decision and fault, or no fault, by both parties in a suit—especially in a case such as this where no actual crime has taken place.

"Sir Rastus, I find that you have not met the requirement of providing sufficient evidence that Henry has plotted to smear your family name. However, you have made your point that your surface area is yours to control. That said, this archeological dig is important to Roacheria. I here-by grant permission for this dig to begin."

The expression on Sir Rastus' face revealed what he wanted to say, but he remained silent. His supporters showed anger in their eyes as well. Relief flooded through me and those who supported me.

"Henry, even though you are exonerated in this matter, I still require you to pay all costs, just as they were laid out in your original proposal. As soon as these funds are delivered to my chambers, and then sent on to Sir Rastus, your project may begin.

"Sir Rastus, the expert you retained to do an initial study may be an active part of the project if you wish. You may observe at a distance if you so desire, but you may not interfere in any way. Enforcers will be on pod to see that you don't. No other spectators will be allowed to trespass on your surface area.

"If no evidence of an ant colony is found, well then, that's that. If evidence of a colony is found, then Henry, as part of his project, may erect a memorial museum as he wishes to do. Sir Rastus, you may charge the public to enter your surface area to see it, but you may not charge more than one credit unit for any adult creature. Youth of any species shall be able to enter with an adult free of charge.

"This judgement may not be appealed by either side. Once I have dismissed this assemblage, you will all leave in an orderly fashion. No violence or any public display of disagreement with my judgement will be tolerated.

"You are all now dismissed!" The Chief Enforcer left the chamber.

Raisa and her mother were seated right behind me. Raisa threw her appendages around me in joy. I returned her embrace. "I knew you would win," she whispered.

"Please, come with me," I asked her. "You've never visited Meadow Commonwealth. I would really like for you to see it."

"Of course," she said. "Mother will come, too."

Many creatures pressed around us with broad smiles, pats on the thorax, embraces, and whispers of congratulations. With glares in their eyes, Sir Rastus and his crowd filed out of the chamber.

One of my mother's fellow Board Members handed her a satchel. "For the fees," he said.

All the way out, roaches quietly pressed credit notes of varying denominations into the sack as she passed by them. It was bulging before we got to the street where hundreds of roaches lined each side of the way we must walk. All along the way, roaches who were strangers to us continued to come up to my mother and push credit notes into the sack. It was overflowing by the time we reached the edge of the city.

Our enforcer friend fell into step beside us, followed by two others as we left the city behind. "We'll escort you safely home," he said.

The words, "Thank you," were woefully insufficient.

Preparations for a feast were already underway when we reached the Common Building. Mother and three others went into our home to count what had been collected. I took Raisa and her mother on a brief tour. I had never felt so happy in my life.

When we reached the edge of the pond, Raisa's mother said, "I think I'll go back to the Common Building and see if I can help."

Raisa and I looked at each other. At the exact same moment we both said, "Will you make a mating promise with me?" and then stopped and also at the same moment said, "Yes!" We laughed, tumbled into the tall grass near the pond and embraced each other.

"As soon as possible," I said.

"But I would like it if we lived at my home."

"I can do that," I said, "and I will never abandon you!"

Walking pod in pod, we went back to the Common Building. We did not need to make an announcement. Everyone could tell we had made a promise to mate by the looks on our faces.

Mother delivered the required fees the following morning. What had been given to us was more than enough for the archeological project and any building we wanted. We decided that when the time came, we would advertise that any creature who wanted to visit the memorial should stop by Meadow Commonwealth first and receive the one-credit-unit fee from the extra given to us until it ran out.

One week into the dig, the soil samples showed that lower-layer soils did indeed lie on top of upper-level soils over a half-a-square d-unit area. The archeologist Sir Rastus had hired for the inquiry actually apologized to our group for his lack of knowledge.

After another week of excavation near the center of the area, one of the diggers fell through a weak spot at the bottom of the pit into what had been the lost colony's main tunnel. But there were no cheers—only reverent silence.

Sir Rastus appeared the following day. "Well, I see you found it. Just so you know, my father once told me that his grandfather told him the mound was leveled about a hundred season cycles ago when the plastic ran out. The place was stripped of anything valuable before it was leveled. You won't find any artifacts."

He left us to the project—never interfering or inspecting the site again.

Raisa and I mated a time frame later. She laid our first egg right on time and it hatched on schedule: a son. When family and friends arrived to share our joy, Raisa said, "He'll have neither an ant nor a roach name. He shall be called Unity."

Friends traveled to Fire Colony 2 and packed up all my notes to bring to a comfortable "office" chamber in Raisa's home, where I completed my draft, and then began translating it into Roach, so it could be published simultaneously in the Combined Colonies and Roacheria.

Sir Rastus was not entirely correct about a lack of artifacts in the Lost Colony. While there was nothing Sir Rastus considered "valuable", items of everyday life were found, many of them definitely made by ants. The findings reflected the ordinary life of the ants who had lived there before their mass murder by Sir Ragnar's warriors. A small chamber of archives had survived all those season cycles.

The records showed that a group of scouts had found the plastic deposit. They had come from a colony deep inside Roacherian surface area where their plastic mine was nearly depleted. They then led a group of 200 surviving families from that dying colony through roach areas, undisturbed.

They doubled their numbers in the first generation and again in the second. A census had been taken only one season cycle before Sir Ragnar's warriors invaded. The colony numbered 1,595 members at that time. Every name was etched into strips of polished metal which were hung along the walls of the entrance tunnel. A few side chambers were excavated as replicas of ant domiciles at the time the colony lived. A meditation chamber was built just outside the entrance.

Eleventh Time Frame 18, 1 C.C.I.

Dara arrived two days after the victory over the roaches at South Dairy Colony 1. She was assigned to live with the family right next to Duncan's domicile, temporarily. He continued his messenger job;

she was assigned to aphid care. They were together from the time they got through with their work until Duncan's mother said it was time for Dara to leave because she was tired and wanted to go to sleep.

Duncan got a message from Master Daeira on their sixth day together, asking him to please stop by because she would like to meet Dara. When the two arrived, Master Daeira had herb tea and honeydew-sweetened grain cakes ready for them. She embraced them both before gesturing to her eating surface.

"These grain cakes from the harvester ants are delicious—especially when thickened honeydew is spread on them. Please, help yourselves."

They exchanged pleasantries for a while. Dara talked about her family.

"Duncan, and Dara, too, actually, I have a favor to ask."

"What?" Duncan asked.

"I've been invited to visit the Intercolonial Council to relate our story, but I have not been feeling well lately. I guess the season cycles are catching up with me. I wondered whether the two of you would go in my place."

The young adults stared blankly.

"I've been told it's about a quarter time frame's travel from your colony, Dara. You wouldn't go all alone, of course. You'd probably stay there several days and then come back here. So it would be less than a time frame all together."

Duncan finally found his voice, "Of course, I would, but, Master Daeira, what caused this illness?"

Daeira smiled. "Oh, not a big worry, really. I'm just very tired and our physician has suggested I take a long rest."

Dara said, "I think I would enjoy a bit of travel. After all my life—so far at least— was lived in one place, until I came here. I think it would be wonderful to see other areas before settling down for good."

"And we would have plenty of time to talk as we traveled," Duncan added.

The two of them left South Dairy Colony 1 two days later. They had made their promise to mate by the time they got to Central

Harvester 12, and they spent a full time frame meeting with small groups of colony representatives. They had asked for smaller groups because they felt awkward about talking to more than 100 at once, so it was over a time frame before they returned to South Dairy 1. Dara's parents and some of their closest friends came with them from South Dairy 50 to be part of their mating ceremony.

The pair went to visit Master Daeira as soon as their friends and family were settled in guest homes.

Daeira received them with great joy, but Duncan thought she looked weaker than before they had left.

"I have something else to tell you," Duncan said as they sipped their tea. "I do want to keep training with you. Dara and I have talked about it a lot. I feel very right about it—being a spiritual guide and having a family."

Master Daeira smiled. "Duncan, you already know everything you need to know. Essence will complete your training. I couldn't be more content."

Master Daeira danced with joy at their mating celebration on the 20th day of Thirteenth Time Frame of that antstoric season cycle. Less than a quarter time frame later, Master Daeira's essence left the physical world.

The final entry in Rashad's journal was written in Ant, not Roach. These are his words in the best translation possible:

To the ants of this colony—13th day of Eleventh Time Frame, 33 O.R.

There are things you should know now. I suspected when Duncan escaped. But I did not tell Rand. My suspicions proved true when Duncan came back. I knew then that our end was coming. He tried to hide the spark in his eyes, but I could still see it. That light of hope spread through the colony. But I didn't tell any of the warriors or Rand. Several times recently, I overheard a specific day. I do not know exactly what will happen, but I know it means our end. And I have not told Rand.

My options are these:

1. *You will succeed. You will have your vengeance and in your view, I am guilty of many things. By all your ways, I should, and will most likely be extinguished.*

2. *If, by some lucky happenstance, I make it back to Roacheria, your success will become my fault in the eyes of Rand and Sir Ragnar. He will find me guilty of treason. He will command one of his warriors to bite me into small pieces (a slow and agonizing death) or he will be "merciful" and send me to the mantis compound.*

3. *I leave in the darkness of this night and escape into the wilds. I learned from those who watch over the grasshoppers which wild plants can be eaten and which are poison, so I will not starve. Perhaps some predator will get me and I will be its food or food for its young. Or maybe Essence will allow me to die of old age. Eventually, we will all feed either fly larva or the earth anyway.*

I still find Master Daeira's statement, all those season cycles ago that roaches have no essence, to be insulting. We are not all lacking in compassion. You saw, in the beginning, how hard most of us work and struggle just like you do. Sir Rainart listened to me and allowed you to live and let your young have plastic. (I had to give up a lot to get you that concession.) But I think I can say with certainty that Sir Ragnar has no compassion.

I will take my chances with the night and the wilds. May I never see any of you, or any of my fellow roaches, again.

I am sorry for the part that I had to play in your lives all these season cycles.

Rashad

OTHER BOOKS IN THIS SERIES:

The Chronicles of Henry Roach-Dairier: To Build a Tunnel, 15th Anniversary Edition

In *To Build a Tunnel*, the first book of the original trilogy, Henry narrates the story of his great-grandfather and two other ants who were tricked by roaches into building better tunnels in Roacherian plastic mines. The ant colony realizes too late that its members have been forced into slavery. South Harvester Colony 45's Council would prefer to solve the matter diplomatically, but are prepared for war.

ISBN 978-0-975341-01-8

The Chronicles of Henry Roach-Dairier: New South Dairy Colony 50, 15th Anniversary Edition

New South Dairy Colony 50, the second book of the original trilogy, opens with Henry as a nymph, in a coma after ingesting a bad combination of medicines in his physician-father's lab. His ant grandfather, Anthony Dairier, decides it's time to straighten out his grandson. He reveals to Henry the details of his own life: the war and the emotional pain which resulted in his dedication to the ideal of the experimental ant/roach colony, New South Dairy 50.

ISBN 978-0-975341-02-5

The Chronicles of Henry Roach-Dairier: The Re-creation of Roacheria, 15th Anniversary Edition

The Re-creation of Roacheria, third of the original trilogy, tells the title character's own life. The adult Henry is an enigma. Most members of New South Dairy 50 consider him too roach-like, even after he outgrows the high jinx of his youth. Influential roaches consider his ways of Antism, and the fact that he is of mixed variety, dangerous to their power structure. Hatreds dating back to the days of Henry's ant great-grandfather rise again in an attempt to destroy him and the community he seeks to build—one dedicated to the continuation of Antony Dairier's dream. Henry and his supporters realize that if the two species cannot come together in true peace, they will bring themselves to the same end as the Duo Pods—extinction.

ISBN 978-0-975314-03-2

Order any of these titles through the author's website: www.authorsden.com/deborahkfrontiera or through other online outlets, searching by ISBN number. Copies may also be obtained through any bookstore using Ingram distribution.

www.ingramcontent.com/pod-product-compliance
Lightning Source LLC
Chambersburg PA
CBHW070452260626
47161CB00004B/1276